WARNING

This book contains sexually explicit scenes and adult language. It may be considered offensive to some readers. This book is for sale to adults ONLY.

* * * * * * * * * * * * * * * * *

Please store your files wisely where they cannot be accessed by underage readers.

Other Books by Carla Coxwell:

<u>Devil's Advocate BBW MC New Adult Romance Series</u>

When Kristie comes home from college, the last thing she is expecting is her world to be turned upside down by the appearance of her step-brother, Gray. Gray is rash, impulsive and breaks the law. Kristie's mom asks if she can try to befriend Gray, in hopes to get him on the straight and narrow. The plan backfires, however, as Kristie finds herself falling for Gray. Is it possible he feels the same way? The connection between them threatens to tear down everything Kristie has ever held dear.

<u>Fifty Recipes For Disaster New Adult Romance Series</u>

Trying to win a competition for best chef is cut-throat business. Kiara Sands has just won the opportunity of a lifetime. When she arrives at Fission, she has no idea just how much her life is going to change. She's immediately introduced to Jenny Foster and Robbs Martin, her competitors in the cut throat competition. The only thing Kiara finds more distracting than Robbs' hateful attitude is the handsome executive chef, Paul Weston. It doesn't help matters that Paul is quite taken by Kiara, and showers her with more attention than he gives her competitors.

iii

Star Bright New Adult Romance Series (This series follows "Fifty Recipes For Disaster New Adult Romance Series")

Torn between her feelings for her agent, Jon, and Rich, a charming bad boy who has ties in the movie industry, Jenny finds herself working through her own past to try to get a grip on her present. As she struggles to learn the lesson that in Hollywood not everyone is what they appear to be, Jenny tries to become a person that she can be proud of. Will she be able to find love and success in Hollywood? Or will she be dragged down by her past forever?

Obsessed Bounty Hunter Romance Series

Jacqui Schneider couldn't help it. Every time the memories of her family's brutal murder haunted her, she had to escape. The only thing that could replace her sorrow was sex...and lots of it. Depressed and with no goal in sight, Jacqui continued on with her self-deprecating lifestyle until it all changed one day. Uncle Max, an old family friend, appeared unannounced. Jacqui was astonished when Uncle Max revealed a secret to her about her father. From those few words, Jacqui's world turned completely upside down. She really didn't know her own father. In fact, she didn't even know much about Uncle Max, except that he visited them for a few days at a time over the years.

Get the latest update on new releases from the author at:

https://www.carlacoxwell.com/newsletter

This book is Part Two of the "<u>Torrid Exposure New Adult Romance Series</u>"

Book 1

April is finished with school and ready to build a career. Coming from a well-to-do family, she has decided to reboot her life completely. With family scars too deep to mend, April craves a fresh start. But the past is harder to shake than April ever would have imagined. At the center of it all is Bennett, an old family friend who is the heir to a billionaire media mogul company. Bennett and April haven't been able to stand each other since they were kids. But as the world shifts, the two of them discover the past might be the key to their future.

Book 2

April is shocked to find Bennett kissing another woman. What takes her even more by surprise are the sudden feelings that swell up in her at the sight. As April struggles to figure out where she stands with Bennett and resolves to stay away from him, her father falls ill. April toes the line between taking care of her father and not getting involved with the family's company. Will April be able to stay on top of everything going on in her life and be able to keep her head on straight? Or will family ties drag her down past the point of no return?

Book 3

April has discovered her sister's darkest secret that has kept their relationship on the rocks since her near-fatal car accident. After learning of her father's death, she suddenly feels as if she has lost her one ally in her family. All she has left is her promise to her father that she will make things right with her sister, Spencer. As April refuses to give up and dives head first into discovering the past, she also falls deeper in with Bennett, the billionaire heir to a far reaching media corporation.

Book 4

April's world is rocked when she discovers the truth behind the night of her accident. Her sister, Spencer, has deep secrets of her own. Both involve a man they have known since they were kids – Kevin, Bennett's father and the owner of a billionaire media corporation. April is determined to help her sister break free of Kevin's clutches and repair their relationship. She wants to help Bennett see that he can stand on his own two feet without needing to bow down to the whims of his father. Can Bennett protect his father without losing April?

Book 5

With Spencer's daughter, Aria, missing and Kevin hot on their trail, April feels as if things have flown completely off the rails. After Kevin lies and tells Bennett that April was kissing Anderson, she finds herself struggling to plan out her next move. Will Bennett help her work against his own father or will he be more concerned about the company? April must put the pieces of her life story together before it is too late

to take down a mad billionaire and his lust for power
but will the target on her back prove to be deadly?

A New Adult Romance Series

Torrid Exposure

Book Two

By Carla Coxwell

Copyright Revelry Publishing 2017

Table of Contents

Chapter One

FOR A few seconds, the fact that some woman is kissing Bennett does not register with me. Emily is babbling in my ear but I don't hear her. I just feel a surge of emotions that leave me feeling breathless.

The woman ends the kiss and tilts her face slightly toward him as he is looking down at her but his expression is blank. Emily tugs my arm hard, asking me something. I don't want to see anymore.

"Hey," Emily cries out, "who is that chick he's making out with?"

She is so loud that even over the music, Bennett hears her. At the last second, as I turn around to tug Emily away, he looks up. I feel his eyes land on me but I am already facing away from him, anxious not to speak to him. I can't even sort out what I am feeling right now.

My goal is to blend in with the crowd. Emily has gotten trashed so quickly that part of me just wants to pile her into the car and take her home. But she is having fun and I don't want to be the sort of best friend that puts my own needs before hers. I decide I'll take her down by the docks and hope she likes being down there instead.

The band is in the middle of playing an incredibly loud song. We are close to the stage and the music makes my eardrums thrum. Emily says something to me but her voice is lost in the music.

We are halfway across the square when suddenly someone yanks on me. Emily exclaims something I can't hear and I turn around. Bennett is looking down at me. He says something but I merely shrug. His words are taken away in the music, lost in the crowd. He tries shouting this time – I can tell by the way his mouth moves – but I can't make anything out.

He looks frustrated. Emily is bobbing to the music, oblivious. He motions over to the docks, where I was heading anyway. I nod and together, the three of us try to make our way through the crowd. Once we get through the worst of it, we are in front of an ice cream store and we stop.

"I didn't know you were here," he says to me. "I didn't see you."

"Here I am," I reply.

I am aware that Emily is nearby. Even though she is drunk, I can't imagine her not picking up on some of this. She is on her phone now, looking engrossed. I realize I should probably stop her because she might drunkenly text Adam.

"You looked angry with me and when I saw you storm off –" someone jostles into Bennett and he practically falls into me, "Stephanie saw you."

"Who the hell is Stephanie?" I reply, sounding more irritated than I wanted to.

"The girl I was with. Anyway, she saw you and I wanted to speak to you–"

"So, what, exactly? If she saw me, and you're with her, why are you here?"

"We haven't spoken since that night," he says to me, lowering his voice so I strain to hear it. "Don't you think we should?"

"Why? It's pretty clear you're already seeing this Stephanie person."

His features darken, "Why don't you let me explain before you decide you know what's going on?"

The song ends. In the few seconds of silence we have before the next track will kick up, all I hear is the murmuring of the crowd. Someone next to me has come out of the ice cream shop with a huge ice cream cone. The bright blue color of the ice cream distracts me for a moment as I debate what to do.

"April?" Bennett presses.

Suddenly, I realize that Emily is not near me. Alarmed, I look around.

"I have to find Emily," I say to him. "Do you –?"

A song kicks up, startling me. Even though I can hear Bennett where we are, I need to find Emily. She is drunk and a mess of emotions and can't be alone right now. Whatever this man has to tell me, about us, or Stephanie, can wait. I don't want my best friend out there, drunk and alone.

I move past Bennett. Our shoulders brush together and even though the touch isn't on bare skin, I still flinch. I quickly walk away from him, heading off down the pathway where Emily might have wandered. She had just been on her phone, after all, and maybe she wanted to call Adam away from all the noise.

I leave Bennett behind and try to find her. On the way, I ask a few groups of wandering people if they have seen her. In the third group, a tall, lanky looking man nods.

"Saw a girl like that head down to the docks. I think she was crying."

I take off in that direction as my heart is pounding although I don't know if it is because of Bennett or Emily. The docks are almost empty - since the sun has set, there is no one sitting out and no one trying to clean their boats. I see her almost instantly. She is at the end of dock number five, looking out at the water.

I jog up to her. She doesn't seem to hear me. I can tell by the way her shoulders are moving that she is crying to herself.

"Em?" I say slowly, not wanting to scare her.

It takes a few seconds for Emily to turn her tear-stained face to me. Her hands are empty.

"What are you doing down here?" I ask, relieved that she isn't hurt. "You scared the hell out of me."

"I was going to text Adam," Emily replies, her voice sounding hollow, "but I knew it was a bad idea. So I came here. I threw my phone in the water."

She's going to regret that when she sobers up, I think to myself, but I merely nod my head and stand next to her. It is an oddly cold night and the wind coming off the water is a bit chilly.

"Do you want to go home?" I ask her.

She shrugs. "I think I'm drunk."

"You are. It's okay, though, I'm here." I try to smile at her and she gives me a tiny smile back in return.

"I've been thinking," Emily says, and she slurs the ends of her words slightly, "about my dad. About how sick he is… in the head. What if I end up like that?"

"You won't."

"We don't know that though, April. We get a lot of stuff from our parents. What if… what if that's why I can't figure out what I want to do with my life? I'm too fucked up."

"Emily, you know that isn't true," I tell her and turn her away from the water. "Let's go home, okay? No more of this."

I can tell she wants to tell me more but I think the best thing for her now is to get her safely home and in bed. She is swaying, as if the wind is going to knock her over. I grip her hand tightly and we leave the dock. Emily is silent the entire time. We get in my car and I make a mental note that I am going to have to pick up her car tomorrow.

The drive home is silent. Emily falls asleep almost instantly, which leaves me to thinking about Bennett. I think about how this Stephanie woman kissed him so easily. Who is this woman? Where did she just magically appear from, going on a date with Bennett?

I know I should be furious but after taking care of Emily all night, plus trying to figure out what my sister, Spencer, is up to, I just feel exhausted. Emily lets out a loud snore next to me as I wait at a red light. In a couple of days, I have the yacht launch with Anderson. I need to be preparing for that, not dwelling on what is going on with Bennett and me.

Emily stirs a little but doesn't wake up. I glance at her as the light turns green. I think back to her life. She has never told me before that she worries she will end up like her father. How long has she been worried about that? It is hard to see her so upset over losing Adam. I am glad that she blew off some steam tonight but it is going to take time to get her on her feet again.

I manage to get her awake and back in bed without any issues. She falls asleep almost right away. I close her bedroom door and head to the kitchen. I go through the process of staring in the fridge, closing it, going to the cupboard, and then opening the fridge again. Part of me is starving and another part of me is ready for bed.

Unsure what to do, I end up staring at the same box of instant mashed potatoes for what feels like ages.

Finally, in the silence of the apartment, my mind goes back to Bennett. He did come after me, wanting to talk. That counts for something – maybe. He was still there with this Stephanie woman, letting her kiss him. But he's always been a playboy. Even *I* know that. Maybe it is just my own mistake for letting myself get caught up in him.

"It's for the best," I say aloud to myself, hoping I believe it. I mean, wasn't I just thinking that the two of us were on different paths? Things wouldn't work out for us anyway. So, if he is going to be dating someone else, it isn't any business of mine. We never made anything concrete or future plans together. Maybe we just slept together to get rid of all those years of irritating, sexual tension. Now we can both move on.

But even as I think this, I wonder why my chest feels so hollow.

Chapter Two

The band is setting up on the stern of the yacht. From here, the saxophone glints in the bright sun. I am hoping it cools off once the sun begins to set. At least the yacht is air conditioned. I step inside the main cabin and put my camera equipment on one of the tables.

Everywhere around me is a bustle of activity. The yacht is being decorated; the food is being prepared and the staff is making sure everything is in order. I sit down on one of the chairs and double check my equipment. It is something I do when I am nervous.

"Great, here you are!" Anderson's voice rings out.

I look up and see him crossing the cabin toward me. He is looking well-polished today. His blonde hair is slicked back and his suit looks great on him. He has a nervous energy, probably because he is really trying to prove to his father that he can run a successful operation, from creating, building and launching the yacht. His nerves rub off on me and I feel myself growing nervous too. This is my first major job and I don't want to mess it up.

"Hey," I say to him, "you ready?"

Anderson bobs on the heels of his feet. "Sort of. We had a couple of staff call in sick so we had to try to find last minute replacements and I had to make sure the menu had something for everyone plus I am hoping that going out into the ocean for a little while is okay –" he stops suddenly. "Ah, you meant just generally, didn't you?"

"I did," I reply with a small laugh, "but it's okay."

"How are you doing? Everything set up?"

"Yeah, I should be all set soon. You wanted me near the entrance, right? To snap photos of the guests arriving?"

"Yes, yes," Anderson replies, twisting his hands nervously, "I want photos of all the guests arriving. They are going to look very glamorous. That is the sort of image I want to portray. Once we set off, you have free reign of the yacht to walk around and take the best pictures you can."

"Great. Well, good luck tonight."

Anderson nods and heads off toward the kitchen. I watch him go and then move to the bow of the yacht. I try to quell my nerves. I want this to go as swimmingly as possible, even if I run into someone I know. These photos have to be great. If I do a great job, then I know Anderson will talk about me to other potential clients. This could easily be my big break.

I take a deep breath and get ready.

<<◇>>

I am about thirty minutes into the arrival portion of the evening. Anderson hadn't been kidding about the type of people showing up to this. He has invited the elite of the elite which is, in a way, incredibly smart. If there was anyone who would want to buy a yacht, it is the millionaires and billionaires of the city.

I've been working non-stop since the first arrival. I want to do a combination of shots tonight - glossy photos of the party and some a little more in-depth... ones that tell a story. Anderson might find them interesting but I know I can use some of the more in-depth, personal stories for my portfolio. I want to have a variety so possible clients can see all the different things I can do.

For some reason, I have been hoping to see Spencer. I can totally picture her here at this event. It is right up her alley. She always embraced the money we had and liked talking with and felt at ease among this type of crowd. But I want to see her because I am dying to know why she was sneaking around the harbor a few days ago. I have come up with no ideas as to why she was creeping around.

I snap a picture of an older man with a much younger woman and watch them head into the party. I can see Anderson in the cabin, chatting up everyone. Even though he is only a client, I hope tonight goes well for him. He is a far cry from the usual heirs I usually meet, who sit around and wait for opportunities to be handed to them. If my pictures can help him impress his father, then I want to make sure they are the best they can be.

I turn back to my camera, resting on the tripod, and almost flinch. Bennett is coming up the ramp. I can see him behind the current couple stepping onto the yacht. On his arm is the woman from the night before, Stephanie. She is glowing in a dark green dress which clings to all the right places without looking trashy and her espresso brown hair is up in a beautiful bun with a few strands of hair framing her face. Stephanie looks beautiful. I am envious, I realize, as I watch them through my camera lens.

Bennett is wearing a designer suit, of course. I've been used to seeing him in suits my entire life but now, it feels different. My heart is fluttering in my chest at the sight of him. I hate that now that we've slept together, I feel this way around him. It's pointless. I try to remind myself that we have no future together and I need to focus on my job.

Bennett looks surprised at seeing me. It flashes across his face briefly as they pose for a photo. Stephanie has green eyes, I notice, which just takes the dress to the next level. She wears a simple emerald pendant. I take their photo. The two of them move past me. Bennett glances at me over his shoulder but I refuse to look at him.

It is another hour of taking photos when finally, the boarding ramp is pulled up and the yacht is getting ready to set out. I pack up my tripod and move inside to try to get the candid shots that Anderson wants. The room is crowded – music is playing quietly in the background as groups of people are talking and laughing. Champagne is flowing freely and the glamor of it all would knock anyone off their feet, yet this is the life I chose to walk away from.

I push the thoughts from my mind and make my way through the cabin, taking photos. Some people want to pose for more photos and I happily oblige. Anderson wants to make sure everyone looks as if they are having a blast in his photos... the more smiles, the better.

I leave the yacht's interior and move out to the deck once again. The band is set up here, playing soft jazz. Some people are dancing while others are sitting at tables, eating food or chatting. We are heading from the channel out to the ocean now. Above me, the stars twinkle, as if they are winking at me. They look gorgeous and mingle with the smell of the salt water now.

The yacht is lit up like a glittering jewel. I know Anderson is right. Once we get out to the ocean, the yacht will look even more beautiful.

"Staring at the sky instead of the yacht. Makes sense."

I don't turn around. I know it is Bennett. His voice is slightly hostile, as if he is angry at me for some reason. I close my eyes briefly and then raise my camera, taking a photo of the band.

Bennett's face appears in front of my lens. I lower my camera and look at him.

"What?"

"Is that any way to talk to a guest?" he asks me. "I mean, you are working the party. So, a little respect would be nice."

I sigh, "Again with this?" I ask him, remembering taking his photos in the office.

Bennett shrugs. "Why not?"

I raise my camera and take a photo of him. It reminds me of the one I took of him at the office – the one of him looking irritated. He had thought I deleted it but I still have it, saved on my computer.

"Gross, delete that."

"Sure," I lie.

"I didn't know you were working this event," Bennett says as the band behind him strikes up another jazz tune.

"Yeah. Working is the key word here. I need to get back to it."

I go to move past him but he grabs my hand. The touch of his skin on mine brings me up short and I find myself stuck next to him.

"Are we going to talk about this?"

"I'm working," I repeat, "so, no."

He lowers his voice. "You know what I'm talking about. Why are you being this way?"

His eyes are looking directly at me. They are dark and I can't read the expression in them. I see us, entwined, on that bed in the guest room. But I shake my head and pull my hand away.

"You're the heir to a billionaire fortune and a media corporation that covers the world," I whisper to him, "and I just gave up everything I was tied to with my family. I'm broke. I have nothing but this camera, do you understand? We slept together. That was it. Nothing will work between us."

I take a step back from him, suddenly out of breath. Bennett is looking at me with an expression on his face I cannot read. He wants to say something, I can tell. His hand clenches mine for a brief moment.

"There you are," Stephanie says as she appears from nowhere and grabs his other hand. "Lost track of you." She turns to face me. "Talking with the photographer?"

"Yes," I reply, finding my voice. "Wanted to take a shot of you two again, if you don't mind. Your dress is stunning."

"Oh, thank you," Stephanie replies to me, looking pleased with herself.

She poses with Bennett and I snap the unwanted photo. Then I turn around and walk away quickly, not wanting to see them together.

<<◇>>

"This looks great. I can't wait to see the larger shots," Anderson says, flicking through the photos on my camera.

"Thanks," I say sincerely. "I'm glad you like them."

He hands the camera back. It is past two in the morning and everyone is tired. The yacht docked thirty minutes ago and the last of the guests left and now I am finishing up, ready to sleep for a million years.

"Hey, thanks again for everything," Anderson says to me.

"Did it go well?"

"I think so. Guess we'll see in a few days once everything hits the press."

"I'll send you the photos in the morning so that you have some for the website and press first thing."

"Thanks, April." He pauses. "Really… for everything."

I wave to him and step outside, toward the ramp. The air, like the past few nights, is cold for the summer and I have forgotten my sweater yet again. I walk down the ramp and through the dock. The area is still full of activity but once I get to the shops, it is quiet. I let myself soak up the silence. It is nice after the noise of the party all night.

As I head to my car, I stop short. Someone is waiting for me there. Even though I can only see the outline, I know instantly it is Bennett. I feel a surge of irritation since I thought I made it as clear as I could that there is nothing for us to talk about.

I march toward him. He hears my feet on the pavement and looks up at me.

"What the hell are you doing here?" I demand of him.

"You said you were working earlier."

"And?"

"So, I wanted to talk to you when you aren't working," he replies in a condescending tone.

"I said all I have to say," I reply, unlocking my car and putting my things in the back seat. "There's nothing else."

I turn around and almost jump up. Bennett has moved in front of me. He stands there, very close, and looks at me. The only lighting we have is from one of the parking lot lights. It hits the right side of his face and leaves the other half in shadow.

"Did you mean it then?"

"What?"

"What you said. About us being too different."

"Why do you care? I've seen Stephanie kiss you. I saw you two tonight. Why are you bothering me?"

We stand like this for a few moments. My breath is coming quickly even though I don't mean for it to.

Bennett is staring at me, as if he is trying to figure me out. Part of me wants him to kiss me. I want it so badly that I can practically feel his lips on mine. But I don't move.

Finally, he takes a step back, breaking the spell between us. He runs his fingers through his hair, looking irritated.

"Dad set us up. Stephanie is the heir to some grocery chain… Halbert's."

"Are you serious?" I reply. Halbert's is probably the biggest grocer in the country.

"Yes. Listen, Stephanie and I… there isn't anything there. Stephanie agreed to be seen together because it looks good to investors. The heirs to Dad's company and her father's company dating," he shrugs. "Looks like we could do joint ventures one day."

"So, you're telling me this is all about business?"

Bennett moves close to me again and this time he is slowly shaking his head. "April… everything in our families is about business. Surely, you know that."

"Yeah, well, I told you already. That isn't my life anymore."

I brush past him and open my car door. Bennett is staring at me. I can feel his eyes on the back of my head. But I don't want to look at him. I feel my heart pounding in my chest at the information about Stephanie. So, it means nothing. But quickly, I shake my head… it doesn't matter if it means nothing. It doesn't matter if they are dating just for show. That isn't my life.

"April," Bennett says again, this time firmly. "I told you. Stephanie and I have no feelings for each other. We do this for our parents. For the company."

At this I turn to face him. "So, what? I'm supposed to be okay with that? What about all the other girls I have seen you with over the years. I'm just supposed to forget them?"

"I'm not asking you to forget them. I'm asking you to talk to me about what happened with us the other day. I'm not asking you out, for fuck's sake, April. I just want to talk about this."

For some reason, this stings me. I suppose that I had been assuming that Bennett wanted to ask me out. His words are meant to comfort me but they only end up making me feel more confused and wounded.

"We slept together. I told you this," I tell him. "We slept together and we got out whatever… sexual tension we had since that night by the pool. That was it. Our lives are too different for anything else, Bennett. You know that too. What would we do? You come here and tell me Stephanie is just some girl you are dating for the company. I'm supposed to be okay with this? You're so out of touch with real feelings."

"Oh, and you aren't?!" he snaps. "What, you think because you severed ties with your old life, you know more than me about what my true feelings should be?"

"That isn't what I meant –"

"I wanted to talk to you about what happened because it doesn't make sense." Bennett is irritated now – we are falling back into our familiar roles. "What happened between us? We spent all the time fighting and bickering and then we sleep together and everything has changed. You feel it too so stop being a bitch. What do we do next?"

I contemplate a retort but get into the car instead. My door is still open so he can hear me when I look up at him.

"We don't do anything, Bennett. We go on with our lives."

I slam my car door shut, unsure if I am making the right decision. He stands there as I turn on the car and back out of the parking spot. Even though we fought, I feel as if Bennett is as lost as I am. Trying to accept the fact there might be something underneath the surface of us sleeping together is too much to take in. For me, even if there is, it doesn't matter. It won't work out.

For some reason, however, it seems to be causing Bennett to struggle. I tell myself it doesn't concern me. He can figure it out by himself. There is no future for the two of us.

I repeat this to myself a few times as I drive home but I am not sure if it sinks in.

Chapter Three

The coffee machine beeps and I pour myself a fresh cup. I have been up for a couple of hours, going back and forth with Anderson through e-mail about the party photos. I am tired. I didn't sleep well during the few hours of sleep I did get after I got home.

No matter what I did, all I could do was lie there and think about Bennett. It was foolish and silly but I did it anyway. By the time I fell asleep, I dreamt about Spencer, hiding in shadows, holding her secrets close to her heart.

The coffee smell helps wake me up a little. I pour some creamer in it and am stirring it in when Emily steps into the kitchen.

"Good morning," I say to her, trying to ignore the fact she looks like a mess.

Her hair is up in a messy ponytail and she is still in her pajamas. She has bags under her eyes but her face is glowing.

"I got a job!" she announces to me.

"Really?" I say to her, surprised. "That's fantastic! Where is it?"

Emily turns her back to me to open the fridge. "Just some office downtown. Filing paperwork. Nothing special."

"What sort of office?"

"Nothing exciting," she replies, pulling the milk out of the fridge. "How was the event last night?"

I frown slightly, wondering where Emily is working but don't know how to press it without making her upset. Her emotions are all over the map lately. Instead, I tell her about the event. I omit anything to do with Bennett. With everything else going on, I still haven't told her about what happened between the two of us. Emily had been too drunk to remember we had run into Bennett the other night.

When I finish, she is almost done with her second bowl of cereal. "Well, that sounds fun," she says. "I mean, Anderson will totally love the photos. He'll probably recommend you to everyone he knows. It'll be great. Maybe you can cover these types of events full time and once you have steady clients, you can work on your other stuff on the side."

"That'd be nice," I admit, thinking about how great it would be to have steady clients.

"What if you have trouble finding work?"

"Guess I'll have to get a side job," I reply, although the thought makes me bummed out. "But I'm trying to stay positive."

Emily finishes eating and stands up, taking her bowl over to the sink. I watch her as I sip my coffee. Something about her is off but I can't pinpoint what.

"I'm going back to bed," she tells me. "Talk to you later."

I realize after she left that she was avoiding my eyes. Part of me wants to go after her but what would that accomplish? Nothing, I realize. Whatever Emily is hiding, she clearly doesn't want to talk about it.

I head back to my room and sit down at my computer. My phone is blinking with a missed call. I wonder if it is Bennett as I unlock my screen. No. It is a missed call from Spencer, of all people. She has left a voicemail. Part of me doesn't want to listen to it but I force myself. Maybe it is about the fact that I trailed after her at the harbor a few days ago.

"April," her voice comes through the other end and I can tell instantly something is wrong. "I'm at the hospital with Dad. He... he had a stroke. I don't know if you," her voice catches, "if you want to come by, I just... I wanted to call you. Okay. Bye."

I am left holding my phone, feeling stunned. I shove my phone in my purse and grab my car keys, heading to Emily's door. I knock hard on it and she opens the door, confused, looking almost guilty.

"Dad had a stroke," I tell her and her hand goes to her mouth in shock. "I'm going to the hospital."

"Let me come with you," she says without a pause. "I just need to get dressed."

I nod but each second it takes Emily to change feels like forty years. In reality, it is just a couple of minutes. She has combed out her hair and put on jeans and a baggy t-shirt. She grips my hand firmly.

"Let's go."

I nod and together, we take off for the hospital.

The first person I see is Spencer. She is in the small waiting room, flipping through a magazine too quickly to be actually reading anything. She seems to sense me and looks up. She stands up at the sight of Emily and me. I hurry over to her.

"What happened?" I ask.

Spencer shakes her head, as if she is trying to focus. "Mom and Dad were going to the country club this morning for breakfast with friends." Her voice is shaking yet steady as if she has repeated this story to someone else already. "They got into the dining hall and Dad suddenly… apparently he just fell over. They called 911 and Dad has been… he's been out of it ever since."

I feel as if all the breath has been sucked out of me. I try to picture it but my mind turns up only blank images. I can't imagine my dad just falling over like that.

"Can I see him?"

"Mom is with him right now –" Spencer starts but I brush past her to go see him.

His room door is ajar. I nudge it open and stick my head inside. Mom is bent over Dad, whispering something to him. I open the door fully and let Mom see me. Her eyes widen briefly in surprise. She looks as if she has aged ten years in a couple of hours.

"April," she says to me.

"Mom."

I step into the hospital room and go to Dad's side. He is fast asleep. The machine keeping track of his pulse beeps next to him. It is jarring… a sudden reminder that if the room is ever truly silent, my father is in trouble. Outside, I hear a nurse talking to Spencer and Emily.

"I didn't think you'd come."

"Mom," I reply, "now isn't the time for that."

She looks at me for a long moment. I briefly wonder if she really is going to start a fight with me about the family right now. But her shoulders sag and she looks back at Dad.

"I guess not," she mumbles.

Together, we keep Dad company for a little while. Finally, a nurse comes in and tells us that the doctor is coming in to look at Dad again and we have to leave the room. Mom puts up a fight but I leave the room without a word… there isn't any point in trying to fight with the hospital staff. If it means they can figure out if Dad is going to be okay, I'll wait out in the hallway.

When I come out from the room, I see just Emily. She is watching something on the tiny TV and stands up when she sees me.

"How is he?"

"I don't know," my voice sounds hollow. "He's just… sleeping, I guess. The nurse said they don't know the extent of the damage yet."

"April, I am so sorry," she says, gripping my hand. "I can't imagine…"

"Thanks," I reply, trying to hold back tears as I look around the room. "Where's Spencer?"

"I don't know. She stepped out, I guess. Maybe she was hungry?"

"I'll be right back."

Emily tries to say something but I want to find Spencer. I pass by my mom, who has come out of the room now, and walk down the hallway. I turn down another hallway toward the main elevator doors and step inside.

Is it stupid to be concerned about following Spencer right now? Maybe. But at the thought of my dad in that hospital bed, I realize I'd rather focus on Spencer and whatever she may be doing instead of worrying about my father.

I take the elevator down to the main lobby and step out, looking around for her. I don't see any sign of her. I take off across the floor toward the main doors and walk outside. It is hot this morning. The sun is burning down on me as I leave the overhang and head off toward the side parking lot.

It is there that I find her. She is speaking to Kevin, of all people. I am surprised to see Bennett's father here. I watch them and notice that Kevin has his hands in his pockets, like Bennett always does. Spencer is crying but also looks as if she is fighting with him. She is gesturing wildly as Kevin just stands there.

I haven't seen Spencer fight with someone other than myself in a long time. After the accident, all we did was fight. Before she went to study overseas for college, she seemed too mellow to bicker and argue.

At one point, Spencer turns away from him and I flatten myself against the wall. Some people glance at me because I'm sure I look like a nut. But a few seconds later, Spencer walks by me. I reach out and grab her on a whim. She turns around, probably to yell at Kevin, but sees me instead.

"What are you doing, weirdo?" she asks, yanking her hand away from me.

"Is Kevin coming up to see Dad?"

Spencer's face looks guarded and she shakes her head. "No. He wanted to but…"

"But what?" I press. "Why were you fighting with him?"

"He didn't want to come up with Emily there," Spencer says.

"What? That's bullshit, Spence," I tell her but she takes a step back. "Why isn't Kevin coming up to see Dad?"

"I already told you, April!" she snaps. "I'm going back up to see Dad. Are you done following me?"

She takes off before I can say anything to her. I turn around and look to see if Kevin is still there but he is gone, as if he was just a mirage. Kevin doesn't invite Emily to any events personally but he has never gone out of his way to avoid her. Kevin not wanting to deal with her family simply comes down to Emily's strange father. Kevin wouldn't refuse to see Dad in the hospital just because Emily was there.

So what is Spencer hiding? What was she fighting with Kevin about? Why had she come here to talk to him?

I turn back to go upstairs into the hospital to spend time with Dad. Whatever is going on, it isn't as important as being with my father right now.

Chapter Four

"I heard about your father," the voicemail from Bennett rings out, "I'm sorry."

The message ends as abruptly as it began. I put my phone down on my dresser and curl up in bed, suddenly feeling very alone.

It has been two days since my dad had his stroke. At first, he was showing signs of improvement. Now, however, he seems to be getting worse. The doctors suspect he had another stroke last night. We are all waiting in a terrible limbo to see what my father will be like once this is all over or if he will even pull through.

Emily is in the other room. I can hear her getting ready for her first day of work tomorrow. Anderson approved the photos I sent him and issued me a check. I should be thrilled. But all I felt was empty when I cashed it.

For the first time in two days, I feel like crying but am unable to let it out. I've never been a big crier. Even after the accident while I was in recovery, I cried only once.

But now I can feel the tears getting ready to swallow me up. Bennett's words ring in my ears. I wish he would have said more. But what else could he have said, especially since I was the one who told him there was nothing for us.

I can hear Emily on the phone. She is talking quietly to someone. I focus on the volume of the voice and the way it rises and falls as she walks around her bedroom.

Before I can cry, I fall asleep.

I am dreaming… back in the wreckage of my accident. I am hanging upside down as the rainwater is pouring into the car. I am dimly aware of a searing pain in my leg. I try to move it but it feels as if it is pinned down by something. I turn to the side and I don't see Spencer.

I try to remove my seatbelt but it is no use. My head is aching and my vision is dimming. Everything feels hot. It feels as if the world is ending and that I have somehow gotten stuck right in the middle of it.

As my fingers fumble with my seatbelt, I look up at a voice that suddenly rings out.

"Spencer?" I say but I realize only my mouth has opened – there was no noise.

The windows are all shattered. I can't see anything. I realize we must have landed in a ditch because of the way the water is pouring in. I hear another voice now – two voices… male and female.

I want to call out but suddenly the pain in my leg is so intense that I shut my eyes. I need to…

I wake up in a cold sweat. My sheets are stuck to me. For one wild second, I really feel as if I am back in the car. I yank the sheets off me as quickly as I can and stare down at my legs. My breathing is heavy. My heart rate is fast. I try to tell myself it is just a dream but something about this one has left a metallic taste in my mouth.

I get up and go to the bathroom. The tile is cold on my feet but I welcome it. I splash some water on my face, trying to calm down.

Was that a dream or… was it a memory? I always assumed I had passed out early on after the crash. But if that wasn't true, what if the secrets of what happened to me that night are all in my own brain? What if I just forgot them due to my injuries?

I pad out to the kitchen and fill up a glass of water and chug it down without stopping. Then I pour another glass and sit down on the kitchen table. This time I drink slowly. I try to go over the dream.

Two voices. One of them had to belong to Spencer, surely. She was there, after all, and moved me to the driver's seat before the paramedics came. Who had helped her move me? Who had gotten there so quickly that the paramedics hadn't arrived first?

I can feel a headache starting. I am missing
something. It is like my brain is trying to remember but
can't quite grasp it. I finish drinking the water and I curl
up in bed. This time, I can't fall back asleep. Instead, all
I can do is lie there and relive the accident.

I am surprised to see Bennett at the hospital the next
day. He is in the lobby, staring at the vending machine.
I don't see Stephanie with him. I hesitate, wondering if
I should go see him. I decide that since we are heading
to the same spot, I might as well go over there.

"Hey."

Bennett looks up as he pushes the button for a
chocolate bar. "Hey back."

"Didn't expect to see you here," I remark, shifting
my purse underneath my arm.

Bennett's light blue eyes fall on me for a few
moments before he bends over to grab the chocolate
bar. "Been here for an hour."

"Really?" I ask in surprise.

"Dad asked me to stop by. He left for London this
morning and didn't get a chance to see him."

"Oh." It is all I can say. I am not sure if I want to
tell Bennett that Kevin was here yesterday, bickering
with Spencer.

"Come on." He gestures toward the elevators.

I trail after him. My head is still hurting and I feel exhausted. I didn't fall back asleep last night but instead watched TV for some distraction. The elevator doors close in front of us and Bennett glances at me.

"You look like hell."

"Wow, thanks."

"Your father is in the hospital, April. No one is expecting you to look like a super model."

I nod, unsure of how to reply. The elevator doors glide open and we step out onto Dad's floor. We walk in silence as Bennett unwraps his chocolate bar and practically inhales it.

"Haven't eaten?" I ask him.

"No, no time." He hands me a quarter of the chocolate which is already nibbled on. "Want this?"

I realize he is joking and it comforts me. It feels like how we used to be, before things began to get messy between us. Mocking each other, fighting with each other – that seemed natural.

"No, I'm okay," I reply, "I don't want your disgusting germs."

He grins at me as if to say that we've shared more than that recently. We enter the small waiting room in Dad's wing. Spencer is there, clutching a book tightly in her hands. Mom is asleep in another chair, her chest gently rising and falling. When Spencer hears us, she looks up. Her eyes widen a little at the sight of me, as if she can't believe that I have shown up to see Dad.

I sit down next to her and Bennett gives us space. He pretends to be interested in a morning talk show.

"April," Spencer says in a low voice, "hi."

"How is he?"

Her face is colorless and she gives me a tiny shrug, "They… not good. They're saying things don't look too good. We're waiting to see if he wakes up… so we can talk to him. He was improving, you know?" Her voice catches.

"I know." I mumble, once again fighting down the rise of tears building up in me.

"Now, they aren't so sure… with this other stroke, they're afraid it could have done damage he won't be able to come back from."

I feel as if a boulder is hitting me directly in the gut. After the initial stroke, the doctors had felt positive that he would make a full recovery with enough time. Now that he has had another stroke, it feels as if the positive energy we had all been trying hard to keep going was quickly deflating.

I nod and lean back in the chair. Spencer goes back to pretending she is reading her book. Bennett is pretending that he cares about what is on the TV. I can't pretend to care about anything. All I can think about is Dad in here, sick, and growing worse.

While I never felt close to my family, I still don't want to see my parents sick. My relationship with my mother has always been a little messy and my relationship with Spencer is fraught with tension and history, but it was always different with Dad. Even though I didn't want to work with him and didn't want any of his money, I still got along with him the best. He accepted my choice tacitly, unlike my mother and Spencer.

Sitting here in this hospital waiting room, where everything feels artificial and sad, I can't help but feel terrified by the prospect of losing him. I feel his spiritual presence in my corner, which gives me some comfort. The bag of mixed emotions confuses me.

My chest constricts so hard that I wonder if I am going to have a heart attack. I stand up suddenly and Spencer looks up at me.

"I have to use the bathroom," I say quickly.

I take off down the hallway, and am blinded by the tears that are rapidly filling my eyes. There is no way that I want to cry in front of Spencer, my mother and Bennett. I had been doing so well holding everything in. Why does it have to hit me now?

I turn a corner and stumble into the bathroom, shutting the door behind me. Luckily, it is a single stall so I don't have to worry about anyone coming in. I lean against the sink and stare up at the lights. The bathroom blocks out the hospital noises. It is as if I have stepped into a small tomb.

The tears are coming now and I don't bother to stop them. I grab some bathroom tissue and try to scrub the wetness from my face but my eyes just keep overflowing. Finally, I give up and rest my head in my hands and let them out as quietly as I can. In this tiny hospital bathroom, I cry until it feels as if my entire body is empty.

Afterwards, I rinse my face clean in the sink. My cheeks are tear-stained and my eyes are red. I am desperate not to have them know that I have been crying. For some reason, I feel the tears will give something for my mom to lash out on. How can I cry when I gave up the family? I can almost hear her words now.

As for Bennett and Spencer, I just don't feel like exposing myself to them like this.

I finish and look at my reflection. In that moment, I don't feel as if I know myself. It is as if someone else is staring back at me. I wonder vaguely if I am losing myself in everything that is going on.

But I have been gone long enough. I pull my hair out of my ponytail in hopes it will cover my face a bit more. I open the bathroom door and collide directly into someone.

Bennett's hands come out and steady me. I look up and he is looking down at me. His hands are on my shoulders. For a brief second, I want to throw myself in his arms and cry. But I remember what I said – how different our lives are.

I take a step back. "What are you doing?"

"Had to use the bathroom," he says but I know he is lying – I know he has come after me.

"Okay. Have fun," I mumble quickly, moving past him.

Bennett grabs my hand. The touch makes me feel a million different things. Before, I would have snatched my hand away and told him off. Now, I want to turn around and hug him. I want to feel him holding me. Maybe I am just being selfish. So instead, I just turn to face him.

"April…" He trails off and looks unsure, something I am not used to seeing on him.

"I have to get back, Bennett."

I remove my hand from his and head back to the waiting room.

It is three hours later when I am finally able to see my father. He has woken up but visitors are only allowed in one at a time so as not to overwhelm him. Mom goes in first and is in there for a long time. Spencer, Bennett and I wait quietly. I don't know why Bennett is still here. He could go home whenever he wants.

Spencer goes next. I offer to go in with her but she says no. Mom came out of Dad's room crying. She didn't say good-bye to us. She just left.

Bennett and I sit in the waiting room in silence. I am holding a tissue in my hand and ripping it into small pieces trying to calm my nerves.

Finally, I can't take it anymore and I look over at him, "You don't have to be here, you know."

Bennett turns away from the TV and looks at me… I can't read his expression. "I thought I could go in with you when you see your dad. My father wants to see him too, after all."

I bite my bottom lip. Part of me *does* want Bennett to be there with me when I see Dad. The other part of me doesn't want to show any weak emotion around him. In the end, the urge to have Bennett there wins out and I give him a curt nod of my head.

It feels as if ages pass before Spencer comes out of the hospital room. Her face is pale. I stand up right away and walk over to her.

"How is he?"

Her bottom lip quivers and she looks away from me, "He's having a hard time retaining information," she finally says. "The nurse says it might go away or… get worse."

She walks past me, saying good-bye to Bennett as she heads toward the elevators. I watch her go. Her shoulders are hunched over and her head is bowed. My throat grows dry. I am suddenly afraid to see my father.

Bennett looks at me expectantly. "Ready?"

I nod as he follows me into my father's room.

Chapter Five

The room smells of antiseptic with a sour scent lingering underneath it. There is a game show playing on the TV. The volume is turned so low that I can only hear every other word. The windows are drawn and the room feels as if I have stepped into the middle of the night. The other side of the room is covered with gift baskets, balloons and flowers from close friends and people from his company.

My father is propped up in his hospital bed like a rag doll. He looks shrunken, as if all strength has been sapped out of him. I feel frozen to the spot I am standing in. Bennett seems to sense this and takes a step toward my dad.

"Richard," he says softly, as if my dad is an animal that Bennett is afraid of startling. "Hi, it's Bennett, Kevin's son."

My dad's face turns slightly to look up at Bennett. His eyes are glassy.

"Bennett," he says to him and his voice is raspy. "Come here, come here."

"Your daughter is here too."

My dad frowns, "I just saw Spencer."

I find my voice, stepping forward, "He means me, Dad."

Dad turns his head toward me and looks surprised. Then he breaks out into a big smile and beckons me over. I sit down next to the hospital bed and Bennett sits in a chair next to me. It feels so odd to be sitting by my father in a hospital bed.

"How are you feeling?" I ask him.

"I'm fine, dear," he replies, gently taking my hand and patting it, "but what about you?"

"I'm fine," I reply, unsure why he seems so serious about how I am doing.

My father frowns slightly. "You don't have to pretend to be strong, April. I know how much the accident took out of you. And to still be in the hospital… it's awful."

I glance at Bennett, alarmed and even he looks stricken. The fact that my dad doesn't think he is in the hospital but I am for my accident makes me realize just how bad he is. Doesn't he realize he is in a hospital bed himself? I can tell Bennett is going to ask him that same question but I reach out and briefly put my hand on his knee to stop him. I don't want to confuse my dad or get him worked up. Better to let him think it is me in the hospital.

"I'll be okay, Dad," I say, trying to keep my voice from shaking. "The doctors were able to save my leg. I'll have some scarring from the accident though."

"Such a shame. I just wish Spencer had been there with you. I wish you had asked her to take you instead of borrowing her car."

The accident is the last thing I want to discuss here, right now, in front of Bennett. His face is blank, studying my father. I am glad he isn't looking at me.

"Dad –" I say, desperate to change the subject.

But my dad goes on, "If she had been with you, maybe she would have been able to help. She had been taking all those first aid classes, after all."

I frown, "She had?"

Dad nods. "Oh, yes. A town over, I think. She was very excited," he frowns, as if he is hitting a mental roadblock. "I can't remember… I can't remember what town though."

"It's okay. That doesn't matter," I say quickly, not wanting to upset him. "I just didn't know she was taking first aid classes."

"Yes, yes. I don't remember much about them. You should ask her. If she had been with you, she would have been able to help."

I lean forward and ask, "Dad, what would she have been able to help with?"

I hear Bennett make a noise, probably wondering why I am asking him this. But I grip Dad's hand tightly and watch him.

Dad doesn't look bothered though… he just looks thoughtful and says, "CPR. I think she said something about that. First-aid. Moving injured people was another one – wouldn't that have been helpful? If Spencer had learned how to move you, April, she could have gotten you out of the car before your leg got scarred up."

I feel as if the air is being knocked out of me. I nod, unable to say anything.

Dad goes on. "But enough about the accident. Bennett," he says, looking at him, "how is your father doing? Nice of you to come visit April."

By the time Bennett and I step outside the hospital, it is mid-afternoon. The heat is like a blanket, resting firmly and heavily on us as soon as we leave the overhang. I am looking forward to summer ending.

"Are you okay?" he asks me, speaking for the first time since we left my father's room.

"No," I reply, too tired to lie.

He stops, putting his hands in his pocket. "It was hard seeing your dad like that."

A lump forms in my throat. "Yeah. It was like talking to a version of him from years ago."

"April," he says seriously, "when have you last eaten properly? You look terrible."

"I don't remember. I'm fine."

"Come on. Let's have lunch together. I'm hungry too."

I hesitate but only for a few seconds before I agree. I am starving. I also don't want to be alone. Bennett has seen my father so he knows exactly why I am feeling the way I do. I agree to have lunch with him.

We get into his car, leaving mine behind, and drive down the street to a little diner. I've driven past it a million times before but never have been inside of it. Bennett holds the door open for me and I step inside – this place is fashioned after the old diners from the 50's. There are a few people throughout but it is mostly empty. The hostess tells us to seat ourselves and I pick a booth in the back.

Bennett slides into the seat across from me and pulls the menus from the side of the table, handing one to me. I open it but the words seem to race across the page. I am having a hard time focusing. Lack of eating, sleeping, and everything going on with my dad has me feeling as if I have been in a shipwreck.

The waitress comes by and I order water. Bennett orders coffee. She leaves and I look back down at the menu.

"Know what you want?" Bennett asks me.

"No."

"I might get an omelet. Maybe. Wait, they have burgers too…" he stares at the menu intently.

I find myself looking up at him while I pretend to look at my menu. After sleeping with him, one would think that having lunch with him wouldn't be so out of the ordinary. And yet…

"Do you remember that time you threw a birthday party and I was forced to go?" I suddenly ask him. "I think it was your eighth. And you were playing soccer. It was before you found out you really liked swimming. And you were captain of a team and some other kid was the other team's captain."

"Ah, yes. I remember."

"You picked Spencer first. I remember being so mad. Everyone thought it meant you had a crush on her."

"But you knew better, didn't you?" he asks, smirking.

"I knew you did it just to piss me off. No one picked me. I was last and ended up on the other team."

"Are you still angry about that?" he crosses his arms, leaning back in the booth.

"What?" I laugh. "No. I just remember how angry I was that Spencer was picked first. She was always picked first for those things. And then our team lost and I was so mad. Spencer and I got into a big fight afterwards. You always were a dick."

"And now?"

I don't know how to answer his question but I am saved by the waitress coming back with our drinks. Bennett orders an omelet. I have no idea what I want so I quickly pick an order of pancakes. The waitress leaves.

"April, I have to ask… what was up with those questions about Spencer?"

"What do you mean?" I ask, playing dumb.

"I know your dad thought it was back when you had your accident. But you seemed intent to ask him about why Spencer was taking first aid courses."

"I just didn't know that she had," I reply, "so I was curious. Strange to find out something you didn't know before."

Bennett frowns. I can tell he isn't sure if I am telling the whole truth or not. In a way, I am. It is surprising to learn that Spencer was taking first aid courses around that time. It still doesn't make sense as to why she didn't want to be caught with me in the crash. But it does prove something – Spencer had been taught to move injured people. Had she been taught that already when the accident happened? Was that how she had moved me?

It feels as if I am getting all these small puzzle pieces but nothing matches together yet. Spencer creeping around the harbor… Spencer and the other voice the night of the accident… her refusal to tell me the truth about that night… the fact that she had been taking first aid courses out of town.

What did it all mean? And why wouldn't she just tell me instead of sneaking around like this?

"April, hello?"

"Sorry," I say quickly, snapping back to earth, "I'm just really tired."

"Let's eat and I'll get you home."

"My car is at the hospital. I have to take it home."

"Fine, I'll come with you then," he says.

"You're not coming with me back home. I'm fine. I can get home myself."

Bennett shakes his head. "You're falling asleep at the table. You shouldn't be driving. Let me drop you off. I can just call a cab back to the hospital or something."

"We'll see," I mumble.

He's right. I am feeling tired. Everything seems to be drained out of me. We barely speak the rest of the meal. I eat my pancakes and when I finish, Bennett pays for the check and we drive back to the hospital to switch cars.

I fall asleep as he drives to my apartment after I tell him where it is. We are only fifteen minutes away but I am startled when I'm woken up.

"We're here."

I get out of the car. I am expecting Bennett to leave but instead he helps me up to the apartment. I unlock the door and remember that Emily is at work.

"Emily got a new job," I tell him as he looks around. "She must be there. She and Adam broke up… I don't remember if I told you that. Sorry the apartment isn't as luxurious as what you are used to."

He ignores the jab. I open the door to my bedroom and get into bed and he pulls the sheets over me. I am so tired that I feel myself falling asleep already. He says something to me but all I do is grunt. I feel him kiss the top of my head but by then I am already asleep.

When I wake up, the sun is setting and I am thirsty. The apartment is silent. I remember Bennett tucking me in. I don't hear Emily. I look at my phone and have a text from her telling me she is going to be home late. I get out of bed and go to the kitchen.

That is when I let out a yelp – he is at the kitchen table, flipping through one of Emily's tabloid magazines.

"What are you doing here?" I ask him, startled.

"Emily reads this drivel?" he asks me.

I snatch the magazine away, even though I agree with him that it is drivel, and put my hands on my hips. "I thought you left hours ago. Why are you still here?"

"Wanted to make sure you're okay."

"I'm fine. Please go. I appreciate what you did for me but just leave."

"I like your place, actually," he says, ignoring me. "It's cozy. If I gave up my family's wealth, I'd want to be in a place like this. You know, your pictures on my website are really captivating. I'm lucky you took them."

"That's great. Thanks. Go."

"So quick to have me leave?"

I am growing irritated now. When I was falling asleep, I hadn't given any thought to Emily being home and seeing Bennett taking me into bed. Now, however, I don't want her coming home and seeing him here. I don't want to try to explain what is going on with the two of us.

"Yes. Go," I say.

"Why, don't want Emily to see me? Think I might let it slip I know she has a crush on my father?"

My phone vibrates in my hand and I look at it. It is another text from Emily.

"*Going to be home after ten tonight* says your best friend, Emily." Bennett reads aloud.

I groan, "Bennett, just go."

"You shouldn't be alone," he says in a serious tone and in that second I realize he means it.

"I'm fine—"

"So, what do you do around here? You have a TV at least. What are we going to watch?" He strolls toward the living room and for a brief moment I want to throw something at him.

"We aren't watching anything. You're going home. And I'm going to rest."

The TV is turned on now and he's flicking through the channels. "None of these are in HD? Wow. It's like the dark ages in here."

"Well, I don't have Daddy to foot the bill for everything like you do!" I snap, taking the remote out of his hand.

Bennett grins, "Wow, why are you getting so upset?"

"Because I have asked you to leave... hours ago, in fact. Yet you're still here. Don't you have Stephanie or someone to go hang out with?"

"Stephanie is with her boyfriend."

That brings me up short. I turn to look at him. "What?"

"She's with her boyfriend. Are you hard of hearing?"

"No. I just..." I trail off, unsure of how to reply.

"I told you, Dad set it up. Stephanie is seeing this guy she likes but I guess he's broke. She met him in a club one night and has been seeing him for six months without anyone knowing."

"Her father has no idea?"

"None. She wants to take over the company, obviously, and her dad would be furious with her if she's seeing someone like that."

I think about this as I flip through the channels. Stephanie, safely away with her boyfriend, keeping him a secret. Something nagged at the edge of my brain as I think about this. Bennett glances at me and I wonder if he is here because he is worried about me. The thought is strange and I am suddenly aware that we are home alone.

Breaking the silence, Bennett speaks, "I told you Stephanie and I aren't anything."

"Doesn't she feel bad? Seeing someone else while she's with the guy she actually likes?"

He shrugs, "I never asked."

"The whole thing is insane to me," I say. "I mean, it feels like something I'd read in a history textbook, back when royal families arranged marriages."

"I don't know why you're surprised. You grew up in the same crowd as me. Okay, so your family isn't nearly as wealthy as mine," he says to me and I roll my eyes, "but all families like ours have secrets."

"Mine doesn't."

"How can you say that after you found out today Spencer took first aid classes near the time of your accident?"

He's right, of course. Spencer is full of secrets, none of which I can figure out. Bennett is staring at me, waiting for me to answer. But all I can do is give him a small shrug.

"It's a minor secret," I finally say.

Bennett is studying me. Not to back down, I stare back at him, as if I am challenging him. It is strange to have him in my apartment. I never thought I would have him over here. Of course, I never thought we would ever sleep together either.

Desperate to change the subject, I ask, "Stephanie kissed you that night at the harbor. Her boyfriend is okay with that?"

"April, I told you that I have no idea what they've worked out between the two of them. Stephanie cares more about her father's company than her boyfriend if she is going along with my father's idea."

"What about you?"

He leans forward a little, enough that I can smell his cologne and am forced to look into his eyes. Our close proximity makes my head feel light for a moment.

"I'm the heir to my father's company no matter what but I'm not going to piss him off in the meantime."

"Does it make you nervous," I ask him, "to know you are going to be in control of the company one day?"

"No," he replies, cocky as ever. "I have it all figured out. I hired a team to make me look good on social media too so by the time I take over, everyone will like me."

"Like your image, you mean?" I counter.

He smirks at me. "That's right. April, you know life is all about your image and how you present yourself to the world. Everyone has secrets. No one ever shows their true self to the public. It'd be career suicide. Dad has an entire team making him look good all the time. That's just how things are."

"That isn't how things are for me. That's why I walked away."

"One of the reasons you walked away," he says softly.

I flinch and move my head back a little, trying to create distance between us. "What do you mean?"

"I used to think you left because you didn't like the money. I'm sure that's still true. I used to think you still used your family's money to get you through college but…"

"What?" I press.

"I think there was another reason you left your family and the money behind," he finally says. "I just haven't figured what it is yet."

I shake my head, "There isn't," I lie quickly. "I was just sick of living that life. I always felt disconnected."

"I believe you. You always were a weird kid."

"Hey!"

"What, you want me to lie? You always were clearly uncomfortable whenever a lot of money was involved. But I still think there is another reason."

I think back to the accident, turning my face away from Bennett's. Spencer lying and refusing to tell me what really happened that night had been the breaking point. How could I ever look at my sister in the same way again? I had been on the fence about leaving but that had been the breaking point. I don't want to take over Dad's company. I don't want any of their money. I just want to be free... although breaking free is a lot harder than I thought.

Bennett's fingers are suddenly gently underneath my chin, turning my face back to his. Our eyes lock and my entire body break out into goose bumps. His eyes are searching my face as if all my secrets are just waiting to be discovered. I want to pull away. I want him to kiss me. Torn between the two, I stay there, frozen. Even though it is just his fingers touching me, I realize with a jolt that I have been craving his touch.

My resolve to stay away from Bennett because we are too different is crumbling away quickly.

His fingers move from my chin to my cheek, pushing back a lock of hair that has fallen in front of my eyes. His touch is gentle. I wonder how a man that can be so frustrating can also be so gentle with me. I hate the different emotions he can pull out of me. I want to go back to disliking him, but his fingers linger on my cheek. It makes my heart skip a beat.

I find my voice. "There isn't any other reason. I'm asking you again to go, Bennett. I'm fine. I don't need —" my voice catches.

"What?" he says and I am transported to our last time together when he whispers into my ear. "Don't need what?"

"You," I manage to say, "I don't need you."

"Prove it."

Then he leans forward and kisses me. The kiss is soft. He is waiting for me to push him away. But my resolve not to get involved further with him has crumbled. The sensation of his lips on mine is too much to push away. I have been craving it. I am weak for it. Bennett can sense this and his kiss changes. He is kissing me harder now. His tongue slides into my mouth as we kiss.

His hand travels from my cheek to my waist, holding onto me as if I might take flight. My own hands wrap around him, digging into his back as our kisses grow deeper. I had been prepared to never kiss this man again. Now that his lips are on mine, the effect is dizzying.

My hands glide up to his hair now and wrap around it, bringing him in for another kiss. He responds by kissing me hard and gripping my waist. Our kisses are hungry for each other. We have been waiting for this. Our kiss ends and he drags his lips along my neck, kissing in all the right places as my heart races so fast I think it might pop.

Unlike last time together where we took our time, this time we are hurrying. I know Emily isn't due home for a few hours but we are impatient. I can tell in the way Bennett kisses my neck and grips my waist.

"Hurry," I tell him.

"Is that an order?" he says in my ear.

"Yes."

I can feel his grin against my skin as his hands pull down my jeans. He yanks them off and tosses them beside the couch. Then he pushes me gently down, unzipping his own pants. He doesn't remove them. This time he merely pulls his cock out through his pants and moves my underwear to the side.

Bennett slides over me, engulfing me in his arms as he begins to slide into me. I sigh in delight and close my eyes, clinging to him. He lets out a soft moan as my pussy takes his cock in. He is so warm and large that I am frozen, getting used to the sensations this brings to me.

He stays still for a few moments, letting me get used to him again before I wiggle my hips against him. Bennett knows I need him to fuck me. The fact we are both practically fully clothed and fucking like this turns me on even more.

Bennett begins to move slowly in and out of me. His hands wrap around my hair and give it a gentle tug as he moves. I wrap my legs around his waist. Everything is blocked out now. There is nothing else I am thinking about except Bennett inside of me.

Bennett pulls his cock out completely, waits a few agonizing seconds, and then thrusts inside of me. I let out a loud moan in surprise, raising my hips to meet his thrust.

"You like that?" he asks me roughly as he does it again.

"Yes," I moan, "yes."

He does the same movement and I can feel waves of pleasure roll out against my body. Bennett kisses me hungrily as he fucks me like this. It is slow. He is teasing me. I am sweating now in my clothes but I don't care. He thrusts his dick inside me again and pulls my hair at the same time. I let out another moan of pleasure as he does so.

"Please," I hear myself say, "not so slowly."

"Oh, you want it harder?" he teases me, stopping completely. "You want me to fuck you hard?"

"Yes," I beg, "please."

Bennett obeys. He is fucking me now, hard and fast, as I cling to him. I can feel myself on the brink of climaxing. Our lips meet again and kiss hard as he moves deep inside of me. It is enough to send me over the edge. I let out a gasp of pleasure as I climax. He climaxes at the same time as I do. Together, we hold onto each other as we let the sensations roll over us.

As my orgasm finally finishes, I lie back down on the couch as Bennett shifts off of me. I manage to sit up and grab my jeans, yanking them on quickly. He watches me, looking amused.]"What?" I ask him.

"You're scrambling to get your pants on," he says as he zips up his pants, "as if we're off to a race somewhere."

"No, I just —" I wasn't sure what to say, actually. Part of me doesn't want Emily to come home early and catch us. The other part of me is mad at myself for sleeping with Bennett again. And then there is another part of me that wants to hold onto him.

So instead of finishing my sentence, I merely shrug.

"Should I go?" he asks me, as he studies my face.

"No. I mean, maybe," I stumble over my words. "Not sure."

He looks at me closely before standing. "Maybe I should go."

I want to tell him to stay. I want to spend the rest of the night in my bed, watching TV with him. But how can I ask that of him? I already told him that nothing could happen between us again and now something has. To ask him to stay feels wrong. Already I feel conflicted. Bennett can sense this. He doesn't say anything else to me. He brushes past me and opens the apartment door.

In those few seconds, I want to call out to him. I feel as if I have done something wrong although I can't explain what. Does he want me to ask him to stay? What does he want from me? Does he want to stay here and cuddle or something? It seems so unlike him that I don't stop him. I watch him close the door and the silence of the apartment hits me full in the face.

Chapter Six

I end up back in my bedroom, feeling lost. I sit on the edge of my bed and run my fingers over my bedsheets. Things feel as if they are quickly getting out of control.

Now, I had sex with him again, on my couch, no less. I can't shake the feeling he is upset with me somehow. Something in the look he gave me right before he left. I wish he would communicate with me. But Bennett isn't one for communication. What was he thinking?

He made a point to try to talk to me about us that night of the yacht party. That meant something, didn't it? But even if I entertain the idea of him wanting to date me, how could I agree to it? Bennett is going to be running his father's company one day. The lifestyle I had turned down is the one he lives every single day. How could I date someone like that?

Frustrated with myself, I bury my face in my pillow. In the grand scheme of things, it feels as if everything is just a distraction for what is going on with my own family. What if I am focusing on Bennett because it is easier than focusing on my father being so sick?

My thoughts are interrupted by the sound of the front door opening. For one wild, stupid second, I wonder if it is Bennett coming back to talk about things. But then I hear the sound of high heels and I realize it is Emily.

"April, you home?" she calls out to me.

Hoping I look presentable, I leave my room and meet her in the kitchen. I am surprised to see how dressed up she is for work. Her skin is practically glowing.

"Had a good day?" I ask her.

"Yeah, it was great," she replies, opening the fridge to grab a bottle of water. "Some of the girls from the office took me out after work to hang out."

"That's great," I tell her, relaxing a little, "I'm glad."

Emily nods, not looking at me as she takes a sip. I am relieved that she is talking to other people besides me. It will do her some good to meet new people. I want to ask her more about work but she changes the subject.

"How is your dad?"

At the mention of my dad, it feels as if I have to sit down. I sit down at the dining room table, staring at the magazine that Bennett made fun of earlier. I tell Emily how he was, including how he thought it was around the time of my accident. Emily looks stricken when I finish.

"April, what's going to happen? To your dad's company and everything? I mean, does your mom take over?"

I hadn't given much thought of the company.

"No, the board will probably just elect someone to fill my dad's spot. My mom will give her blessing, I'm sure, but you know the business isn't really her thing. Spencer was learning the ropes of the company when I left. She might go work there full time. I don't know."

"What about you?"

"What about me? You know it doesn't have anything to do with me anymore."

"I guess," Emily speaks faster when she sees my face. "I didn't mean it like that. I just wondered if you would go back to the company if your mom asked."

I blink in surprise. "No. I mean, I never really learned anything about it from Dad. That was more of Spencer's thing." I pause. "Why? You would go back?"

"I don't know. Sometimes I wonder what I would do if my dad hadn't sold off the casinos. Would I have gone to work there... learned about the business? But you're right, of course. You bowed out of that life. Sorry... I guess I'm just sort of all over the map."

"Yeah," I mumble, lost in thought. "Hopefully, it won't come to that."

"I'm sure it won't," Emily says quickly, trying to reassure me. "I'm sure your dad will be just fine."

I nod in agreement but Emily has opened a new door to consider. If something does happen to my father, what would happen to the company?

Was it any of my concern anymore?

<<<>>>

"Anderson couldn't stop speaking highly of your work and when I mentioned how we are throwing this big party, he told me I simply had to reach out to you."

I smile. "That's great. Anderson was great to work for."

The woman, Michelle Cash, smiles at me as she looks down at her menu. Late last night, I got a call from her, telling me she wanted to meet with me regarding setting something up for photos. Here it was… my first major reference from a client! I jumped at the chance to meet her for lunch the next day.

"I'm thrilled to be discussing this with you," I tell her honestly, "and for such a major event as well… it's fantastic."

"Our record label only throws these listening parties for major artists. Honey is a break-through star. We feel confident her debut album is going to hit the top of the charts. Naturally, we want a photographer there taking the best photos to generate some buzz for her."

A listening party for a possible brand new major singer sounds like a great gig. I am thrilled that Anderson has recommended me for this. If I keep getting recommendations like this, soon enough I will have enough money to branch out in my photography jobs. I could bypass these mainstream freelance work and start taking risks on some lower paying, more artistic endeavors.

The waitress comes by and we order. After she leaves, I hand my portfolio over to Michelle who flips through it.

"Love this," she says, pointing to a shot of Bennett looking irritated back at the office where I had first taken that photo. "He looks familiar." She studies the photo for a few extra seconds.

"I took some photos for his website," I say to her, "but I think this one really had the best energy."

She nods, distracted by me to study the photo more and turns the page to some of the yacht photos. "Anderson really went above and beyond here. I was sorry to have missed it. I was in China... had a deal going through with a client."

I nod. "Anderson really put his heart and soul into the yacht launch."

"He's so keen to impress his father," Michelle replies. "You know, I'm about twenty years older than Anderson but his energy always impressed me. I know his father quite well."

Something in her tone of *quite well* makes me wonder how exactly she means it… not that I am going to push it.

"Anyway, his father is a bit of a hard ass. But Anderson is determined to make his mark on the company. Admirable." She closes my portfolio. "I like these photos. This is the sort of thing I am looking for at the listening party."

"Great," I reply.

Michelle pulls out a thin folder from her briefcase and hands it to me. "Here are the details. You can review them and let me know if they meet your requirements."

Another job landed! I want to grin like a fool but I am determined to look as professional as possible. I nod, clutching the folder to my chest. Michelle leans forward.

"Now, tell me. What was it like working for Bennett Hunter? His dad tried to buy our company once, back in the seventies… did you know that?"

Great, I think to myself, *I get to spend the rest of lunch talking about the very person I want to avoid thinking about.*

When I stop by the hospital after my lunch with Michelle, my mom is outside of my dad's room. She is talking to someone from the company. He doesn't look familiar but he is so boring looking that I wouldn't be able to spot him apart in a crowd anyway. Mom's face is scrunched up and I can tell she is trying not to lose her patience.

Sensing a fight, I move quickly toward her. I can smell the alcohol on her right away.

"Mom, hey," I say quickly, "what's going on?"

The man looks at me. "I'm Brian Capre. You must be April." He holds out his hand for me to shake although his face doesn't change.

I return the gesture and shake his hand. "Yes, hi. How are you?"

"I'm sorry to stop by to see your father under these circumstances but the board is nervous. We wanted to see how he is doing. With him in the hospital, we have no clear cut leadership and our stock is falling."

Mom looks at me angrily. "Shareholders sending this man to here while Richard is in the hospital, to discuss business!"

Knowing that if I can smell the alcohol on her means that Brian can as well, I grab his arm and lead him away from my mom. My mom sways on the spot a little but doesn't move to stop me.

"Sorry, please excuse my mom. This is a stressful time for everyone," I tell him, hoping my tone sounds blank, like his.

"I was hoping to speak to your father, miss," Brian replies. "It is about the company and while I understand that they are only allowing family in to see him, I was hoping —"

"Sorry, they are strict on that. No business. They don't want to stress him out," I lie quickly.

I am suddenly very worried why a shareholder is here. I have always tried to keep my nose out of my father's business. His restaurants were all over the country but I couldn't remember the last time I had stepped into one. A couple of years back he had started a line of frozen meals in supermarkets. That was the extent of what I knew.

But if a shareholder is here and sees the sight of my father barely knowing where he is or what he is doing… that would be cause for concern.

"That is a shame. I was hoping your mother would be of more help but…" he trails off, letting me know that he knows she has come to the hospital drunk.

I try not to cringe and reply smoothly, "She's been extremely stressed out. I'm sure you understand."

"April, may I say something?"

"Yes, sir."

"April, I understand your father is recovering. But the company needs guidance. It needs someone running it. I have come here to see if your mother would step up to the plate."

"Surely, there is someone else who can take over right now. Someone on the board? Someone my father trusts."

"The man your father has as a *back-up*, if you will, quit two days ago," Brian says and I hope the surprise doesn't show on my face.

"You don't mean…"

"Yes, James has quit, miss."

I bite my lip so that I don't curse. James had been my dad's co-partner years and years ago. The two of them had worked together through thick and thin. Last time I saw James was at the frozen food launch party. He is younger than my dad and at the party, he'd had a pretty wife on his shoulder. Growing up, James was as much a part of the company as my dad himself.

"Why?" I find myself asking Brian.

A strange look crosses Brian's face. It is as if he is trying to recall information about me. Then it dawns on him… *ah, yes*. This is April. Not Spencer. This is the daughter who turned down the money and the company to set off on her flight of fancy of taking photos. The change in his face is instant. He looks at me as if I am a daft child.

"Is your sister around? Spencer, I mean?"

"No," I reply curtly. "Tell me what is going on."

Behind me, I can hear my mom complaining about Brian to one of the nurses. Sensing his time is short before he gets kicked out, he looks back at me.

Looking resigned, he lowers his voice and replies, "Miss, your father's company is in trouble. Declining sales. Your mother's… meddling, for lack of a better word. Now James has quit and everyone is fighting for control. When is your father coming back? He needs to get back to work or this company is in trouble."

He straightens up as the nurse comes over and quietly asks him to leave, explaining that my mother doesn't want anyone from the company around. Brian gives her a smile that looks like a shark about to eat dinner and then flicks his gaze over at me before he turns around.

I watch him go, suddenly feeling very small and without guidance. My head is starting to hurt. My mom is suddenly by my side.

"Can you believe him? The nerve! Even after I told him to go away. What did he say to you?"

I hesitate, wondering what to tell her. But I turn around anyway to look at her.

"He said James quit and the company is in trouble." I pause before adding, "but you knew that…didn't you?"

Mom looks lost. Maybe she is too drunk to deal with this information. I am too sober to deal with it, surely. I move past her and walk toward Dad's hospital room.

"April!" she shouts, snapping out of it to look at me. "If he's awake… you can't… you can't tell him… about James."

I nod before I turn the handle and enter Dad's room.

Chapter Seven

The last thing I feel like doing is meeting Spencer for a coffee. But after the events at the hospital and knowing she is working at Dad's company, how could I not? Mom clearly is sticking her head in the sand. Brian is ready to take over the company… I can just tell by the way he speaks and looks at me.

How could Dad's company be going under? Maybe it is silly of me to always assume the business would be fine. Restaurants are a hard business. Even restaurant chains are no longer safe.

I look down at my hot cocoa, lost in thought, as if I can pinpoint when things started to change. But since I had tuned out from the family business at a young age, I find myself out of ideas of where things had started to go south.

Brian said it has to do with my mother's meddling. My mom loves to meddle. It is part of her nature and drives everyone mental. But Dad always managed to keep her in line. What has she done to the company that left such a problem to the point where Brian has to remark about it?

I still can't believe that James left. My dad's right-hand man, who had a chance to fully take over the company, has left.

What makes things worse is Dad's deteriorating condition. Today, he was distant, slow to respond and got easily confused. The conversation we had where he had thought I was in the hospital due to my accident seemed mind blowing compared to today. He was mostly sitting in silence as I struggled to get words out of him.

"Fuck," I mumble, rubbing my forehead and wishing I had stopped to get headache pills.

"Bad day?"

I look up to see Spencer sitting down across from me. She is holding a cup of coffee and clutching it so hard that her knuckles are white.

"Hey. Yeah, bad day," I reply as she takes a sip of her coffee.

"What did you want to talk about?" Spencer asks, getting right to the point… no more small talk between these two sisters.

I recount to her the entire conversation with Brian. When I finish and take a sip of my hot cocoa, Spencer looks alarmed. That isn't reassuring. I had been hoping that she would have known what was going on in the company and tell me everything is being handled.

"Did you not know any of that?" I ask her.

Her cheeks puff out and then she exhales. "I knew some. I knew James had quit."

"Why did he quit?" I press. "He loved Dad."

"Yeah, I know. But listen, April. Brian is right. The company is in trouble. But I didn't know how bad it was until Dad got sick and I tried to do some of his work for him."

"So you knew some things were bad?"

She looks uncomfortable now but still answers, "Yeah. I mean, you know I've been working at the company since college. My plan was always to work there. So I heard rumors. They got steadily worse the past year. I asked Dad about it one time."

"What did he say?"

"He said not to listen to the rumors… that the company was fine. So, I believed him."

"It doesn't sound as if everything is fine."

"Well, it isn't. After Dad went in the hospital, I tried to step up. Help out, if I could, but not run the company," she amends quickly. "Helping out James. That's when I learned the full extent of things."

"And?"

She shifts in her chair, looking away from me. "A lot of the restaurants have been closing. Mostly on the other coast. Our vibe is old. Outdated. No one wants it.

Profits are down. James wanted to renovate but I guess Dad was going against him."

"Why? That doesn't seem like Dad. He'd do whatever it took to get the company back on track."

"People are blaming Mom," Spencer whispers, as if Mom would appear at any moment.

"Brian did say she was meddling but I didn't know what he meant."

"April," she says, "this isn't any of your concern. You severed ties with us. With the family and the business. And that's fine. I… I get it, why you did it. So, don't worry about the company now. It doesn't matter."

"I can't just… I can't just stop caring, Spence," I protest. "This is Dad's business. He worked so hard on it. How can I just sit back while he's sick and let it all rot out?"

"I'll handle it, okay?" she replies, brushing me off. "I've always been more involved. Don't worry about it. The frozen food sales are still good. As long as we have that, we'll be okay. James is gone because he got frustrated, because he just didn't feel as if anyone was listening anymore."

"You mean Mom," I counter.

Her silence tells me that I am right. I feel as if I am searching for the right words to tell Spencer that even though she is right – the company has nothing to do with me and I severed ties with my family – that doesn't mean I severed all ties emotionally. It doesn't mean I just don't care anymore.

"If I can do anything —" I struggle to say.

"Like take photos?" Spencer replies and I can tell right away by her face that her remark came out harsher than she had intended.

I fall silent. She stands up. Clearly, she has decided that none of this is my concern. Before she leaves, however, I have to ask her one more thing.

"Spencer?"

"What?"

"Dad said… he said that you were taking first aid courses the same time as my accident."

She flinches, as if I have physically struck her. Her eyes harden. She is emotionally shutting down but I stand up as well, determined to follow her.

"I was," she finally replies.

"You moved me, didn't you?" I press. "That night. You learned how to properly move injured people."

"You're being ridiculous," Spencer counters, "I told you. Over and over again. That I can't… I can't tell you."

I grab her arm. I smell her perfume and something about it strikes up a mental image of her from the past.

But the memory fades as quickly as it comes as I stare her down.

"You weren't alone that night," I tell her and the way she widens her eyes lets me know that my dream was right, "and you moved me. You had someone helping you. Someone who held off the fucking paramedics until you got out of there."

"Stop it, April," Spencer hisses through clenched teeth. "I told you to stop looking into it. I know you were following me at the harbor. Stop going where you don't want to follow. Trust me."

She yanks her arm away from me and turns around, storming out of the coffee shop. I watch her go, glancing down at my cocoa, which is probably cold now. Every time we meet, it ends poorly. It ends in us fighting about the night of the accident. I close my eyes, trying to control the way my heart is beating.

Everything feels as if it is sliding out of my hands and making a mess on the floor. My dad. His business. Spencer and her secrets. Bennett and how complicated our relationship is growing.

Bennett. I bite my bottom lip at the thought of him. Would it be crazy to think that he would know about my father's company being in trouble? I don't want to go to his dad, and try to find out information. But Bennett, might know something. More than Spencer will tell me since she is keen to remind me my dad's company has nothing to do with me.

So, even though it is like picking at a scab that is trying to heal, I find myself calling him.

It is now later in the evening and we are back in the guest house. The same guest house where I caught Bennett having sex with that girl all those years ago and the same guest house where we first slept together. Bennett has seemingly moved into the guest house because he doesn't care enough to move off his father's property.

"This really isn't ideal for me," I tell him as I step inside the foyer. "I don't want your dad to see me. He'll just ask me questions and make a big deal out of it."

"As he should. For someone who wanted nothing to do with her family, she sure is asking a lot of questions."

I walk into the living room, throwing my purse on the couch, "I'm so sick of hearing that."

"Someone else is telling you the same thing?"

"Spencer is," I reply. "I didn't realize because I didn't want my family's money that it means I can't care about anyone in my family anymore."

Bennett looks at me, as if he is trying to read my mood. "Do you want a drink?"

"No, thanks."

I try not to admire him, no matter how handsome he looks tonight in a regular t-shirt and jeans. He turns around and goes over to the bar in the living room and pours himself a glass of whiskey. I watch him and in spite of myself, I can't help but notice the way his muscles move against his t-shirt.

"Like I told you before, I used to think you got what you could from your family and then just left but…" he turns back to me and his bright blue eyes are staring into mine. "I don't think just because you don't want your family's money, that means you can't care about them anymore."

I look at him, trying to figure out his angle but there doesn't seem to be one. I relax a little.

"Thanks," I reply, feeling a little unsure of what to say. "He's my dad. I feel like my mother and Spencer just want me out of the way. I don't get it."

"Maybe you deciding the money wasn't for you made them feel bad. No way could your mother turn down that money. Spencer, too. I don't know your other reasons for doing what you did but I'm sure they are more complicated than what meets the eye…" He shifts his weight, suddenly looking uncomfortable. "I wasn't very fair to you about that. I should have been more understanding."

I am surprised at his words. For a brief second, I debate telling him about Spencer lying about the night of the accident but I hold back. I don't feel comfortable sharing that night with him… not yet, anyway.

"Thanks," I say and I truly mean it. "Money was a part of it but not the only reason I left."

Bennett sits down next to me. Briefly, our knees touch and the connection sends shockwaves through me, even though it is such a slight touch. I move an inch away, trying not to get distracted by mental images of our time together.

"You said you were calling me about your dad," he says, clearly not wanting to get distracted either.

I nod and tell him some of my conversation with Spencer. I skirt around some details, like our fight about the accident, and only briefly mention Brian, unsure of how much I want to reveal to him about my father's company.

"I know you're seeing Stephanie and it is just… for show, I guess, but her father is big in that world… supermarkets, grocery stores that hold my father's food. I guess it is a long shot but I thought maybe you heard something. From her. At parties. I don't know. Something Spencer isn't telling me."

"I honestly thought you knew that the restaurants weren't doing so well. I didn't even hear it from Stephanie. I heard it from my dad."

"Kevin knows?"

"My dad knows everything," he replies. "I just assumed… maybe that was silly of me because of how things are going with your family but I just assumed you were aware of how poorly things were going."

"Fuck," I mumble, running my fingers through my hair. "I had no idea. No one told me."

"I heard that your dad wanted to do a heavy remodel of the restaurants with James's ideas but your mom was against it. She didn't like the cost. She kept getting involved and your dad let her. I don't know why he did," he adds quickly as he looks at me, "so don't ask. That's all I heard. James probably got irritated and quit. More people are going to jump ship unless your dad gets better and gets back in control."

"Does everyone know this shit except for me?"

"Everyone probably assumed you didn't care. Listen, April, you can't pick and choose what you want from this life. You can't say you want out and then get pissed off when you don't know what is going on in the business. That isn't how it works."

He is right, of course, but his words bother me. Maybe it is the lazy way he says them, as if he is just pointing out the obvious. Maybe it is that Bennett of all people has to be the one to tell me this.

"Yeah, but my dad is sick. I think I have a right to know what is going on!"

"I think you're rightly stressed out and sad about your father so you are deflecting everything and fixating on the company. But the company has nothing to do with you. That's a fact. You gave all of that up when you dropped out of your father's will and inheritance. It's your mom's problem and Spencer's issue now, not yours." Bennett goes on in that casual voice of his, "Maybe you think you can control what is going on with the company because you can't control your father. But it isn't any of your business, April."

"My dad worked hard on the company and now it is falling apart," I protest.

"And so what? So what? If the company goes out of business, then it doesn't affect you," Bennett replies, sounding slightly irritated now, "so don't stick your nose in it. Take care of your dad. Hang out with him. Help him. But the business has nothing to do with you."

The words sting only because deep down, I know Bennett is right. I am focusing on the business to distract how concerned I am for my father. Even so, I don't want to admit he is right. It is an old knee-jerk reaction to Bennett. Whenever he hits a nerve, the last thing I want to do is let him know that he has hit it. I stand up, suddenly feeling foolish for coming here to talk to him.

"What, you're leaving now?" Bennett asks, "Why? You know I'm right, April. You don't have to get pissed off at me about it. I told you what I knew about your father's company. I understand you care about your family. But you left the money behind and the business. So why keep harping on it? Just let it go. It has nothing to do with you."

"I have to go," I mumble, suddenly terrified I am going to cry.

I turn and leave the living room, hoping to get out of the guest house before Bennett stops me. But he grabs my arm and spins me around.

"April, why are you being—"

Suddenly, I am crying. The tears come fast and furiously before I can even utter a word. Bennett looks surprised. I cannot remember if he has ever seen me cry before. Probably not since we were kids and I skinned my knee or something.

He hesitates for only a moment before he gingerly wraps his arms around me. I don't pull away. Instead I allow him to hold me as I cry all over his t-shirt. He runs his fingers through my hair gently, not saying anything.

We stay like this for some time. It is strange to be crying to Bennett, of all people. But there is something oddly comforting about it as well, as if he knows how I am feeling.

After a few minutes of this, my tears slow down enough that I can speak without having to gulp for air, and I look up at him. "Sorry. You're right. The company… it doesn't have anything to do with me. I'm just scared of losing my dad. He's been the only one who understood my point of view. He wasn't upset at me deciding to go my own way. If he is gone then…" I shrug a little, feeling pathetic. "There will be no one in my corner anymore."

"I'm in your corner," he whispers so quietly that for a moment I wonder if I imagined him saying it.

Our eyes lock but he doesn't move at all. I can feel his heart beating steadily underneath my fingertips pressed against his chest. How is he not nervous? Whenever I am near him it feels as if my heart might pop from how quickly it beats. It has always been like that, I realize. I have always been jumpy around him and on the defensive. Is it because I always felt something toward him? How can Bennett be so calm?

His words stir something in me. Memories of us as children appear in my mind. Watching him swim at our house, as my father and his father discuss business. Spencer listening in on their conversation, eager to prove her business sense. Me, off to the side, reading a book. Bennett splashing water on me *accidently* just to bother me. For some reason, this moment is vivid in my memory. I remember yelling at Bennett to stop and my dad rushing over to see what was wrong.

I don't know why it is this moment, of all moments, that I think of. We were just kids. But this memory repeats throughout my life. Small moments of Bennett teasing me and making me angry. Yet every time he came over, I found myself close to him, wanting him to notice me.

"Are you okay?" he whispers, bringing me back to the present.

"Fine. I'm just emotional," I say, rubbing my eyes quickly. "I'm sorry. I came over here because I wanted to find out what's going on with my dad's company. But you're right. I can care about my family but I have given up my right to start meddling in his business. It was just a distraction so I didn't have to think about how sick my father is."

"It's natural to want a distraction," Bennett says softly yet firmly. "I'm not trying to be a dick. But wondering what is going on in the company isn't your problem. You're just worried…"

"What?"

"I think you're just worried if the business goes under and your dad is gone then everything you have from him, you've lost. But that isn't true. Your dad will get better, April."

His hands move to mine and he is holding them. There is nothing suggestive about this. He isn't trying to seduce me or come onto me. I can't help but look up at his eyes. They have shifted shades of blue again. I am lost in the dark blue eyes of his – like stormy seas. I can feel myself being dragged under.

"I'm scared," I say quietly, the first time I have said this since my father had his stroke.

"I would be too," Bennett replies. "It's okay to be scared. It's natural to be scared."

I allow him to pull me in for another hug. I try to push the scary thoughts out of my mind. I try not to think about my dad, sick in the hospital, with the business struggling. Instead, I focus on my breathing. I try to breathe in sync with Bennett. My urge to flee the guest house has faded. I feel unmoored, unsure of where to go. I could go back to the apartment and see

Emily… yet I have to admit that being comforted by Bennett is the strangest and nicest sensation I have felt recently.

"Do you want some tea or something? I think there's chamomile. Remember when my mom thought that just drinking chamomile was a fantastic diet idea?"

"Yeah, she practically ended up in the hospital because of the hunger pains," I reply, thinking about his mother, Sophia, thin as a waif and still constantly trying to lose weight.

"She stored it all here. Come on."

He doesn't let go of my hand and instead leads me back through the foyer to the kitchen. There are more of his things in here and I look over at a pile of textbooks, puzzled.

"What's that?"

Bennett glances over at them as he pulls down the kettle from a cupboard, "Nothing." When he sees my look, he shrugs, "I found them in the main house. Old textbooks. I just wanted to flip through them. Maybe I can find something for someone on my team to write an article on. For my website."

I sit at the breakfast nook, pulling one of the textbooks toward me. "How is that coming, anyway?"

"Fine. Like I told you earlier, Dad wants me to have an online presence for whenever I take over the company."

A thought strikes me. I wouldn't have been able to ask him this before but with everything that has unfolded between us, I feel as if I can now.

"Does it ever bother you that you can't go out and do what you want to do? For a job, I mean. Have you ever considered not taking over your dad's company? Or was that always a given?"

Bennett pauses, clearly taken aback by my question. It is probably the first true question I've asked him since we have become closer. Everything we have discussed has either been about my issues or his love life.

"Sometimes I think about what I would do if I didn't have the money," he finally says. "When I heard about you leaving the family's inheritance behind, for instance."

I am surprised. "Really? I remember you being a dick about it when you found out."

"I didn't understand how you could have everything handed to you on a silver platter and turn it down. At the time, I didn't understand how you couldn't want all the money and a chance to work at your dad's company," he said with that old confident swagger in his tone that I knew so well. "But still."

"So what changed?"

"I kept thinking about how you were always taking photos. It was so annoying. At every social event, there you were, taking your picture… it was like 'go away'.

Something about it bothered me. At first I thought it was because I had imagined you thought you were better than everyone else. And after the accident, everyone treated you like a wounded bird."

"Tell me about it," I reply. "You think I didn't notice how everyone hovered around me? Especially when everyone was worried I was going to lose my leg."

Bennett holds up his hands. "Okay, message received. I know I sounded like an asshole. Your accident was no joke. I know that. That's because I realized I was angry at myself. You always knew what you wanted to do. You were brave enough to leave the life you didn't want behind and strike out on your own. I could never do that."

"But you said you thought about it."

"Yeah, what would I do if I told Dad I didn't want to take over the company… I realized I didn't know. All I've been taught is business. There is nothing else I have cultivated on my own."

"You like to swim," I point out.

"That leads nowhere."

"Forget about making money," I reply. "What would you do if you didn't have to worry about money?"

Bennett hesitates. I can tell there is something he would do but he is nervous to tell me. The kettle sounds off at that moment and he pours the boiling water into the teapot.

"I thought about going into wood-working. Construction, maybe."

It is the last answer in the entire universe I thought I would hear from Bennett. In fact, I grip the counter, as if it can keep me up from falling over.

"You can make money in that," I say quickly, trying to hide my surprise.

"Let me show you something."

He leaves the kitchen and heads toward the stairs. Intrigued, I follow.

"I know what you're thinking," Bennett says to me. "I should move off my dad's property and get my own place. I'm sure he'd have no issue with it. I guess it's easier just to stay here. Dad has been teaching me so much about the company that driving across town to meet up with him seems like a waste of time."

"This is the nicest guesthouse at least," I reply as we head down the hallway.

"True. But," he pauses for a moment, "feels odd."

"What does?" I say as he stops in front of one of the doors.

"Talking to you. You live on your own. No money to be found. I'm still living on my dad's property, basically waiting to take over his company."

I'm not sure what to say. I hadn't been expecting Bennett to tell me so much about himself. He is usually so private. The fact that he worries about living on his dad's property and wants to get into woodworking is the strangest thing I think I have heard in ages.

"Anyway," he says with a quick shake of his head, "here."

He opens the door.

Chapter Eight

I am staring at shelves filled with lots of small wooden figures. In the center is a table with different tools on it and a stool is next to that. Light is pouring in from the window, offering a great view of some of the guest houses.

Bennett looks at me, not saying anything. Slowly, I walk over to one of the shelves. I pull one of the wooden figures off the shelf. It is of a young girl holding a bucket. I glance back at him, unable to speak.

"Yes," he says to my silent question, "these are mine."

I put down the girl holding the bucket and look at another figure. It is of an old woman, sitting in a chair. The fact that Bennett made these is mind-blowing. It is the last thing I ever thought he would do.

"Lame, I know," he says to me. "Dad doesn't get it. Last summer when I was gone for two weeks, I was out of the country. Dad had a friend in construction and he was giving me a crash course in house building. Isn't that weird? Dad thought it was ridiculous that I wanted to learn how to set up a house. But his friend was cool. We made a small cabin."

My mind is whirling with this onslaught of information. The last thing I want to do is have the wrong reaction. Bennett showing me this is a big deal for him. I don't remember the last time I have seen him look so nervous.

"Bennett, these figures are amazing," I tell him, meaning it as I look at another one.

"Thanks. I'm running out of room. I'm thinking about just throwing them out. I don't know what to do with them. Dad is right. They're pretty pointless."

"What does your mom say?"

"She thinks it's cute," he says with an eye roll. "She has some on top of her dresser."

"These aren't pointless," I tell him. "This is your hobby. Why is that a bad thing? These are great. And you building a cabin? That's even more amazing."

"Why is that?"

"For you to be outside for more than ten seconds, doing hard labor? Never would have pegged it," I tease him.

He rolls his eyes but he is smiling now. "It was pretty fun."

"You're a hands on sort of guy. Never would have thought that about you."

This time his grin was lewd. "Really?"

It is my turn to roll my eyes. "You know what I mean."

He holds out his hand to me. "The tea is probably ready. Come on."

I take his hand in mine and he leads me out of the room. I want to stay longer. I want to look at all of Bennett's creations and understand that side of him. It is a side that I never knew existed. There is more to this man than I ever gave him credit for.

The tea relaxes me. We sit in the living room with the TV on in a comfortable silence. My mind keeps drifting back to the workroom Bennett has upstairs. I try to picture him – alone, hunched over, carving out those small figures. It is even harder to imagine him leaving the country to go make a cabin.

I glance at him out of the corner of my eyes. He is on his phone, scrolling through a webpage. How can someone I have known my whole life have so many unknown things to him? Bennett must feel my glance because he turns his face to me and catches me staring.

"Like what you see?" he says, teasing me.

I turn away from him, back to the TV, trying not to blush. Hanging out with him like this is a new feeling. Every other time we've been together lately, we have either been fighting or having sex. Now, there is no pressure to sleep together. It is as if we are just hanging out like a couple.

The thought is a new one and comforting. As I drink my tea, I feel the most relaxed that I have felt in weeks. That is until Bennett's phone goes off. I look over at him. His face darkens as he answers.

"Stephanie," he says into the phone and I feel my good mood shatter. "No. I can't make it tonight," Bennett says with a pause. "No, I don't care."

His tone with her isn't friendly. I think about the fact that she has a boyfriend that she must care about. In that second, I dislike Kevin more than I ever have in my life.

"Well, I can't make it. I don't know why my father told you I could. No. I'm busy. Go to the event alone. Fine."

He hangs up and runs his fingers through his hair, suddenly looking stressed out.

"Everything okay?" I ask lamely.

"This… phony-dating-Stephanie thing is just irritating me," he says. "At first, I was fine with it. Dad was right. It does look good to have us dating. Well, it makes Dad look good. It's a perfect match. Few other families have the wealth we do and Dad wants to keep it…" he moves his hands in a circle.

"In the family. Like the ancient Egyptian royal families did," I chime in jokingly.

"Very funny," he replies dryly.

I can't help but laugh. I know that I shouldn't. Bennett is obviously irritated with both Stephanie and Kevin. He looks back down at his phone and I grow serious.

"I should go," I tell him. "Sounds like you have a lot going on."

"Nothing fun. She has some stupid dinner party she wants me to go to and apparently my dad told her I could go. I have about ten minutes before he calls me, ordering me to go."

"Is he still out of town?" I ask.

"Yes. Comes back in a couple of days."

I stand up, suddenly feeling like an annoyance. "I'm going to go then. Not that I don't want to hear Kevin unleash his fury on you but I need to get home anyway. I have a record listening party for some artist called Honey that I need to start planning for."

Bennett's phone goes off then and he cringes. "Ahead of schedule."

I want to say a proper good-bye to him. A kiss maybe… something. But he answers the phone before I can say anything.

"Dad, I know," he says right away, "I know. I'm starting to have second thoughts about this fake dating bullshit we have going on with her." He falls silent and I can hear Kevin on the other line, his voice rising and falling.

I can tell that there won't be any kisses from Bennett tonight. Part of me is relieved. But as I close the front door of the guest house behind me, I realize that I have learned more about him tonight than I ever expected to.

Layers upon layers. Everyone I think I had known my whole life is shifting and turning into new people.

Am I changing as well?

Chapter Nine

The listening party for Honey's debut album is underway. I am trying to take a photo of two well-known artists talking in the corner but the place is packed. I am currently pressed against a corner of the room, hoping to blend in so no one will notice me. Unlike the yacht event where the guests basically ignored me, this party is the opposite end of that.

Artists, both well-known and clearly struggling to get noticed, are vying for my attention all night once they see the badge I have showing that I am working for the record company. I take as many photos as I can but I am also hoping for some more natural photos of the party, not just posed shots of famous people.

"Oh my God, are you the photographer?" comes a voice next to me, high pitched. "Can you take a photo and give it to that agent over there?"

I glance at the girl who looks as if she snuck in here and I turn around to avoid her. I move through the crowd. Honey's album is blaring loudly and she's on a small stage in front of the crowd. She has platinum blonde dyed hair and is overly tanned with a wide smile. She is bobbing her head to the music.

I manage to get through the worst of the crowd and set up on the other side, near the stage. I set up some shots of Honey, pleased with how they look. I turn around to see if there is something else worth taking a photo of when I swear I see someone familiar, but they disappear quickly, sucked up in the crowd. No one I know would be at a party like this.

The crowd moves a little and I see the person again. It's Adam. Part of me wants to go over there and punch him in the face. He is sipping a drink and bobbing his head in time with the music. I've known Adam long enough to know he hates the pop music Honey puts out. I suppose he is phonier than anyone suspects.

I take a photo of him. He doesn't see me. I had completely forgotten he worked at a record company. What are the odds of it being the same one that I am working for tonight?

Losing interest in Adam, I spend some more time walking around the venue, taking photos. Part of me is itching to take some shots on the sly, like of the couple bickering in one corner. But Michelle wants to review all the photos and probably wouldn't want to see dark and dirty photos of people fighting at her party. I promise myself that soon I will be able to go out and take the kind of photos that I would actually want to take.

Near the end of the performance, the party isn't as crowded. I think security has removed most of the people who had snuck in. This thinning out of the crowd makes it easier to take photos. At one point, I go to the second floor of the venue and raise my camera, hoping to get shots of people dancing below.

That is when I see Adam again. He is dancing on the floor, arms above his head. I snicker. His dancing is terrible. I try to remember if I have ever seen him dance before but I don't think I have. I take a photo of him, arms up in the air and his mouth closed tightly. Then Adam turns around and pulls a woman close to dance along with him. *Jerk*, I think as he turns the woman around to kiss her.

Then I blink rapidly, as if I have something stuck in my eye. Through the lens, I realize the woman he is kissing is *Emily*. Stunned, I lower my camera and watch the two of them kiss on the floor before dancing together. Her hair is up in a bun, like it was when I saw her earlier today, but her clothes are different. She had told me she was going to visit her father. Instead, she's here.

My feet are moving before I can even think about what I am going to say when I see her. I get down the steps and cross the dance floor, pulling on her arm. She opens her eyes and sees me. Her mouth opens and closes, like a fish. Adam, oblivious to the fact Emily has stopped dancing, is still swinging his arms around stupidly as a new track kicks up.

It is too loud to ask her what she is doing. Instead, I turn and leave the dance floor. Emily follows me. We end up near the front of the building where it is less noisy and more people are talking next to the bar.

"Emily, I didn't expect to see you here," I tell her, trying to sound as if I hadn't just seen her making out with Adam.

"I didn't know… I didn't know you were working this party," she tells me, fiddling with her hands. "I thought it was another party. I didn't ask… I should have asked…"

"Did you get an invite from Adam?"

"No. I was invited but it's because I work… here… with Adam."

My eyes widen. "What? I thought it was an office job."

"It is," she says quickly, "but it's at this record label. In Adam's department. He got a promotion. From someone he met at Kevin's party."

"The party where I saw him hitting on another girl?" I ask her, losing patience.

"April, don't. This is why I didn't want to tell you that I got back together with him."

I think back to her actions and mood recently. She had been short on details when it came to her job but I hadn't thought too much about it, too wrapped up in my own issues. Now it made sense.

"Listen, April. I don't need you to worry about me. I can take care of myself. I didn't want to tell you because of how you'd react. Plus, you have so much on your plate right now, with your dad being ill."

I close my eyes. I don't want to fight with Emily. Not here and not while I am working.

"We can discuss it later," I tell her but she is shaking her head quickly.

"No. Sorry, April, but I am not talking about this. This is my life, not yours. And I'm back with Adam. That's the end of it."

Before I can reply, Emily walks away from me and the crowd swallows her up. I watch her go, feeling like I've been struck in the chest. Different feelings roll through me. I try to grasp onto one but I can't. I feel upset that she didn't tell me she was seeing Adam again. I'm angry at her for being so stupid to go back to a man who was cheating on her. I'm irritated at myself for maybe, somehow, being too hard on her so she didn't feel as if she could talk to me about Adam.

I take a deep breath and head back into the party, determined not to let this distract me from my job.

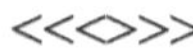

It is late by the time Michelle comes over to me to let me know I can head out.

"Everyone left here are mostly drunk. No more glamorous photos at this point," Michelle tells me. "You can head home, April. Thanks for your hard work."

I thank her, relieved because I have been wearing heels all night and my feet are killing me. I quickly glance around to see if I can see Emily but I figure she must have left already.

By the time I get home, it is after two in the morning. I open the apartment door slowly but there is no need to. Emily is still awake and has the television on. When she sees me, she stands up.

"Hey," I tell her as I set down my camera equipment.

She is fiddling with her hands again but looks determined, as if she is upset about something, "You embarrassed me in front of Adam tonight."

I'm tired and my feet are sore. I want to tell her that I don't care. But I also don't want to fight with her. On the way home, I realized I can't get on her for not telling me about Adam. Emily still has no idea about what is going on in my own life with Bennett. Even though I think it is foolish that she is back with Adam, it isn't my place to lecture her.

"I'm sorry," I reply. "I didn't mean to. Knee-jerk reaction I guess. I just don't want you to get hurt."

"Adam says—" her voice catches. "Adam says that you're jealous."

Of course he does, I think to myself, growing irritated quickly.

"Does he?" I reply.

"He says you're taking out your break-up with Matt on us. That you want me single because you are."

I exhale slowly and say, "What about you? What do you think?"

Emily looks cornered, as if she hadn't been expecting me to bypass Adam's thoughts and ask for her own. Adam, whom I never really thought twice about when they were first dating, is quickly revealing himself to be manipulative. Emily, who is always unsure of herself or what to do with her life, doesn't seem to notice such blatant maneuvers.

"You forgive him, then," I prompt her, "for cheating on you?"

"Yes," she replies. "Everyone makes mistakes, April. Adam was so… so distracted in his goal to get a promotion that he threw away what he and I had to get it. But he sees that now. Things are going to be different this time."

"I told you, Em, that I'm happy for you. If you want to be with him, that's fine."

"Fine," she tells me and then adds, "I'm going to be staying with him for a few days. He's going out of town for a business meeting and has brought me on as his assistant."

I want to groan aloud but I stifle it. I can't believe I had Adam pegged so wrong. He had seemed like a nice guy when they were dating. His true colors are one of a cheater and someone who is quick to manipulate Emily. I want to shake her. Instead, I merely nod.

"Have a good trip."

I head toward my room, hoping she lets the conversation die. She does. I feel as if she had been gearing up for a fight. Maybe Adam had worked her up for one. Adam will want me out of the picture. He knows I don't like him and that I am the one who is not afraid to speak out against him.

I wash my face and brush my teeth and curl up in bed. Even though I am exhausted, my head is spinning. I can't help but blame myself for not noticing that Emily was back with Adam. Even though we are the same age, I have always felt as if Emily is my younger sister. I am supposed to take care of her and watch out for her. Somehow, I have slipped up and now look at what's happened.

Am I being too hard on myself? I think back to what Bennett told me. I worry about the fate of my father's business because it is easier than thinking about how sick he is. Am I distracting myself again by beating myself up over Emily?

After an hour of tossing and turning, I finally fall asleep.

Chapter Ten

I am starting to get used to the scent of the hospital. It is a strange mixture of bleach and recycled air, covered with a strange perfume, as if to try to mask it. As I visit Dad the next day, it strikes me how many different stories are in this hospital. Each room I pass with someone inside it has their own story. Their own struggles. For some reason today, that feels overwhelming.

After a terrible night of sleep, I arrive as soon as visitor hours begin. Spencer and Mom are nowhere in sight. I have no idea what they are doing to pass the time when they aren't here. Is Spencer trying to fix the company? Is Mom drinking more? I feel more disconnected from them than I usually do.

By the time I finally got up this morning, Emily had already left. Her door was ajar and her suitcase was gone. I didn't even find out where she was going or just how long she would be gone. Again, that sense of becoming disconnected struck me as I stood in her bedroom, feeling as if this were somehow my fault.

The nurse lets me in to see my dad. He is sitting up, staring at the TV. The news is playing. His eyes still look glassy and there doesn't seem to be much improvement. I swallow hard, not wanting to cry in front of him. I sit down next to him.

"Hey, Dad," I say, overly cheerful.

"April, you're here. Great. Where's Spencer?" he asks me.

"I'm sure she'll be around later."

"I was hoping that the two of you would come by together. I never see you two together anymore."

"Just busy," I tell him.

Dad is acting almost whimsical now. "You two used to be such peas in a pod. So close, you know? I remember how you used to chase each other around the backyard and come up with all sorts of games."

I remember it too and the sudden thought makes my grip on my chair tighten. Spencer and I *had* been like two peas in a pod. We had done everything together. Even when I felt distant to the material side of things, Spencer and I had still remained close. It wasn't until the accident that our relationship crumbled.

"Yeah, it was fun," I tell my father, "too bad we still couldn't run around the backyard, huh?"

Dad smiles at me, "Isn't that the truth? Spencer was always full of crazy ideas. You two would feed off each other's energy and cause all sorts of trouble."

"You mean the time we were all in Cancun and Spencer and I ran off because she told me there was buried treasure somewhere on the beach?"

Dad laughs at the memory. "A big storm came in and we were all so scared about where you two had gone. We found you two afterwards, hiding out in a cave on the beach. Spencer had somehow started a fire and you were trying to build a shelter."

I can recall the cave. There had been no treasure. And even though I had been scared at the storm coming in, Spencer had remained cool under the pressure. We had gotten lucky and found an old fire-pit in the cave, which she had managed to light with a lighter she had bought for our *adventure* along the beach. Together we spent time huddled next to the fire. I wasn't scared once Spencer had started the blaze. It was just another crazy adventure with my sister.

The memory of the cave and our explorations makes me sad. It feels as if everything before the accident is one fantastic memory of how close Spencer and I used to be. Whatever she is hiding from that night must be important enough to tear our relationship apart. I can't imagine what that could be.

Dad gently grabs my hands and for the first time since the stroke, I see real clarity in his eyes. "April," he says to me, "I know why you made the choice you made. You never were the materialistic type. I know this life isn't for you. I respect that. But that doesn't mean you can't still be close with Spencer. You two need each other. You're two sides of the same coin."

His speaking is low and quiet, as if each word is a struggle but still he finishes up what he wants to say.

I can't speak. I know if I speak I am going to cry and I don't want to cry. Dad pats my hand again and I nod in agreement.

"I remember the night of the accident how you said Spencer had been there. Whatever happened that night… if there is something you aren't telling us or something you need to keep private… I hope that the two of you can work it out. I would hate to think that I am no longer here and you two aren't speaking." His speech is slower now, as if he is running out of batteries.

"You *are* here," I protest feebly. "You're going to get better."

Dad smiles at me and my heart constricts. Suddenly, I lean forward and hug him tightly. His arms wrap around me weakly and he returns the hug. Tears spring to my eyes but I hold back from crying. I don't want to stress him out. I don't want him to see me crying when he is sick.

"April," he finally says, "don't give up on your sister."

I shift away from him and look at my dad. His eyes are growing foggy again. It is as if storm clouds are covering him. I am losing him to the effects of the stroke. The moments of clarity grow smaller and smaller. The fear inside me pumps through my entire body. I want to stay here forever, by his side.

"I won't," I tell him.

"Promise?"

It is a big thing that he is asking me. For some reason, I know Dad can sense that. He doesn't want Spencer and me to drift apart forever.

"I promise," I finally answer.

Dad smiles at me and leans back in bed. It is as if all the energy has been zapped out of him. His eyelids are already closing with the need for sleep. I hover over the bed. I know I need to let him sleep but still I remain. I try to soak him up. I want to remember this moment.

As I leave the hospital room, my thoughts turn to Spencer. How can I try to patch things up with her? I've tried everything under the sun to get her to tell me what happened the night of my accident.

Maybe telling her that Dad wants us to patch things up will be enough. Maybe if she hears what Dad said, she will be more willing to open up.

It is a long shot but I have to take it. For Dad.

That means making a trip back home.

I haven't been back to my family's house in a while. It is technically the same neighborhood as Bennett's but on the outskirts. Even so, our house is still large. There are twelve bedrooms and nine bathrooms. Our pool area is large. There is a garden in the backyard that Mom used to like to read in, before she began drinking more and more. Spencer and I used to play different games in the garden, usually pretending we were fairies holding court.

I pull up through the gate and park on the wide circular driveway. Our house is modern and minimalistic compared to the show of wealth that Kevin has splayed around his mansion. Dad never liked showing off our wealth as much as Mom did.

My heart is beating fast. My palms are sweaty and I try rubbing them on my jeans. It is strange how the house I grew up in can make me feel so nervous. Since everyone parks their cars in the garage, I don't know if Spencer is home. I am hoping Mom has already left for the day.

I take a deep breath and get out of the car. My hands fumble with the key to the house, which feels awkward and heavy in my hand. I slide the key in the lock. It clicks open. I am worried that Mom had the locks changed after my announcement. Dad probably stopped her.

The lock gives way. I open the heavy oak door and step inside the foyer. The house is silent. I have a direct view to the living room from here. I can see one of the pool cleaners outside, bent over and trying to clean the hot tub. I walk into the living room and stop, looking around. Everything looks unchanged. I am not sure what I was expecting… something to mark the fact that I had turned this all down, maybe, as silly as that sounds.

"Spencer?" I call out and hold my breath.

A woman sticks her head out of the nearest hallway. I recognize her from the cleaning crew. She has been working with the same crew for ages and knows me on sight. Even so, she seems surprised to see me.

"Spencer is out," she tells me, "as is your mother." She hesitates before asking, "Is everything okay?"

"Yeah, I'm okay. Thanks. I'm just going to pop upstairs."

The woman nods and ducks back into the hallway. For some reason, I have an overwhelming urge to go to my old bedroom. Did they keep everything the same or has it been cleaned out? It is a good way to kill time to see if Spencer shows up. I am eager to speak to her. For the first time since the accident, I want to try to work on the relationship between us, instead of just staying angry at her.

Up the stairs I go. Spencer and I used to run up and down the stairs and pretend to be chasing each other, pretending to be monsters. We got in trouble once when I fell down these stairs and broke my wrist. The monster game ended then.

I can almost feel the swooping sensation in my stomach of falling down the stairs and landing at the bottom. The pain had felt odd and I was crying and giggling at the same time. I can recall Spencer's worried face, hovering over me, asking if I was okay.

The top floor of the house has all the bedrooms. I walk past the guest rooms. Most of them look untouched. I stop in front of Spencer's room. The door is ajar. I bite my bottom lip and poke my head in. Her bedroom is exactly the same. She painted it pale blue years ago and never changed it even after her favorite color changed to yellow. She has a bay window that overlooks the front of the house. I can almost picture her now, sitting there, with a book propped open in her lap.

My eyes scan the rest of the room. Everything is neatly organized. Everything has a place. Spencer has always been like that.

Part of me wants to go snooping through her room. My fingers are itching to start poking around in there, trying to find out what happened that night. But I can't bring myself to do it. It's wrong. Whatever Spencer is hiding, I can't throw my own morals out the window and start going through her things.

I take a step back from her room and shut her door firmly. Best to get away from the temptation all together.

I turn and walk down the hallway. My room is at the end. The door is shut. My hand rests on the handle, getting a sense of déjà vu. Even though it hasn't been too long since I moved in with Emily, it still feels weird to be outside my old bedroom. I turn the handle and open the door.

The memories smack me in the face. My parents haven't moved any of my things. Maybe they are still expecting me to come home. Everything is exactly as how I left it, including the empty spaces left behind of things I took when I moved out. My bed is gone, for instance, but a bookshelf too large for my small apartment remains. Some gaps are there from books I took with me.

I move over to the bookshelf and run my fingers along the spines of some of the books. Old comforts. Things I used to curl up with. The row with my journals is empty. There was no way I was going to leave those behind.

I stop by my window. From here I can see the front grounds of the house. How often did I stare out this window and frame photographs with my mind? It feels like so long ago. I turn and open my closet. When I left, it was empty. Now there are two boxes shoved in there like an afterthought.

Curiously I move toward them and open one of them up. My breath catches. They are filled with old family photo albums. Who shoved them in here? My mother? Or Spencer? For some reason, I know it was Spencer who did it. She left that photo in one of my boxes when I moved after all.

I pull out the photo album on top and sit on the floor. I flick it open randomly to one of the pages. It is of our family on vacation. Spencer looks to be about twenty here which would have made me sixteen. I try to remember where we were. I have to admit, after a while, all the beaches we visited started to blend together.

In the first shot, Spencer is posing on the beach. Her hands are up in the air and she is smiling. I am in the background but my face is tilted to one side. I am clearly distracted by something.

In another photo, we are all at dinner. Kevin's family is with us. I remember this vacation now. We were in Hawaii. A family friend had gotten married and we all went to Hawaii to attend the wedding. I study the group photo. Mom and Dad are in the middle. I am next to Dad. I cringe at how silly my hair looks, shoved in some weird bun. I probably thought it looked artistic. Next to Mom is Spencer. She looks much more refined than I do. Her face is beaming and she is propping her face on the table with one hand, looking almost like a model. Kevin is next to her. Like always, for an older man, he looks handsome and mature. One hand is wrapped around his wife, Sophia, who looks slightly drunk. His other hand is underneath the table.

Next to Sophia is Bennett. He is dressed in a suit and is leaning back in his chair. His smile is easy and confident.

I turn the page and scan the photos. More of Spencer. I have forgotten how much she liked being the center of attention. More photos of her at the wedding grace the following few pages. In one, she is playfully dancing with Kevin. Her face is tilted back and she is laughing, looking as radiant as the sun.

My chest constricts. I can hear her laugh now in my head, as if I am in the photo. I can't remember the last time I heard her actually laugh around me. It makes me feel sad just staring at it. I turn the page.

Chapter Eleven

"Are you in here?" Spencer's voice rings out.

I feel frozen for a few seconds as she steps into my room. I stick my head out of the closet and her eyes widen at the sight of me. Her hands are filled with folders and a tablet, which she places on top of my old dresser.

"April? What are you doing here?"

"I want to talk to you," I tell her, closing the photo album quickly, "so I came by to see if you were home."

"You want to talk to me?" she repeats, her face now guarded.

I stand up and look at the folders. "Where were you?"

"At Dad's office… trying to plug the holes in the sinking ship," she says grimly.

"That bad?"

She runs her fingers through her hair looking almost forlorn.

"Just a lot to cover," Spencer replies, clearly dodging the question.

"I didn't come here to talk about Dad's company," I tell her, hoping that will relax her. "I just want to talk to you."

Spencer is still looking at me as if I am going to leap at her throat. I realize at this point we both expect to talk about the accident every time we are alone. She studies my face.

"I saw Dad this morning," I say.

Spencer studies me for another couple of seconds and then says, "Want something to drink? We have that cocoa you like."

"Hard to say no to hot cocoa," I reply, following her out of my old bedroom.

We walk down the stairs and go into the kitchen. Everything is perfectly in order. It looks as if no one has cooked in here in ages. Spencer pulls out the cocoa and I get the milk. We make it in silence. For once, however, it isn't a weird silence. It is the silence we used to have together when we were focused on something.

Once the cocoa is ready and I put on way too much whipped cream on top of it, we sit in the living room. We look out at the pool. The cleaners are gone. The sun is high up in the sky at this point.

"Can't wait till summer is over," I say idly to Spencer. "This one is so hot."

"Way too hot for my liking. Dad had been talking about —" her voice catches at the mention of him but she goes on anyway, "about heading up North for a little trip to get away from the heat."

"That would have been nice," I say neutrally.

"Yeah. Anyway… that fell through."

We fall silent again. This silence is a little more awkward. I want to tell her what Dad said but it makes me nervous to talk to her like this. I clear my throat and shift so I am looking at her.

"Dad… he wants us to… he asked for us to… reconnect," I finish awkwardly.

Her eyes widen slightly in surprise. "What?"

"He says that we're sisters. And he doesn't know why we aren't close anymore but he wants us not to forget our bond."

Spencer looks away from me and down at her cup of cocoa. The gesture is familiar to me. Whenever she is nervous, she hides her face from whomever she is speaking to.

I keep going. "What happened to us? We aren't sisters, anymore. I know I walked away from the family. I know you know that I walked away because of the accident. Because I couldn't stand the fact you couldn't tell me what happened that night. Why you lied."

"Are you saying you don't care anymore?" Spencer asks, still not looking at me.

I tread carefully, not wanting to start a fight with her. "It isn't that I don't care anymore. I do. I just don't want us never to speak again because of it."

Spencer finally looks up at me. "April, I'm not proud of what happened the night of the accident. It's something I think about almost every day."

"But whatever the reason is… you can't tell me, right? There was something going on that night that you can't tell me about," I finish for her.

She looks away again, running her fingertip over the edge of her mug. "It's complicated… and easier for everyone if I don't go into it."

"But you understand where I'm coming from, don't you?"

"What?" she asks, surprised. "April, of course I do. Of course I understand why you want to know what happened. It isn't as if I don't want to tell you. I just… can't."

Normally, this is where I would become upset. Instead, I just feel sad. Whatever it is, whatever the reason that Spencer can't tell me, it has to be something major. I can't even imagine what it could be. At a loss for words, I take a sip of the cocoa. The sweetness of the warm drink takes the edge off my nerves.

She shifts next to me. "I know I fucked things up. And they can't go back to how they used to be."

"Dad said we are two sides of the same coin and we need each other," I tell her. "I just don't know how we can start over."

Spencer and I both fall silent again. I am not sure what else to say. I had been hoping if I approached her out of kindness, with Dad's words behind me, something would change. All the times we had spoken before had been out of anger.

"Do you think that…," Spencer asks stumbling over her words, "that we are two sides of the same coin?"

I hesitate before answering. "Yes. But I don't know if we can start over."

"Unless you know the truth," Spencer finishes for me. "I can't. I'm sorry."

I swallow my sadness.

I place my cocoa down on the coffee table and stand up. "I should get home."

Spencer doesn't reply. I walk around the couch and leave the living room. I suddenly want to get out of this house. The memories are smothering me. I feel silly. I feel angry at myself for promising Dad the two of us can patch things up.

I am back out in the humidity now and get in my car. I need to get home and finish sending the photos to Michelle from the record listening party. I fiddle with my car keys, starting my car. Part of me wants to call Bennett. I want to tell him what I know from the night of the accident. I want to see if he knows anything. But as soon as I think it, I dismiss it. Focusing on the accident isn't going to help things. It is just another distraction to forget how sick Dad is.

So, with one last look at the house, I head back to the apartment.

Chapter Twelve

I am dreaming again. This time I know I am definitely dreaming. I am staring at the car. I can see it turned over in the ditch. The rain is coming down in sheets. I can see the outline of my body in the car. Somehow I am in both places. Maybe I have died.

I walk over to the wreckage of the car. The heat coming off of it seems to burn through my skin yet I feel nothing. I crouch down and peer inside. I see myself trapped upside down in the car. I am rolling my head from side to side, trying to wake up. Spencer isn't in the car.

Spurred on by this, I leave the other version of me stuck in the car and wander away from the wreckage. I want to find Spencer. The rain is so heavy that I can barely see anything in front of me. Surely, she couldn't have run off this far?

The farther I walk away from the wreckage, the more the surroundings around me shift. The ground warps underneath my feet, from muddy grass to tile. The trees are vanishing and there is thick fog surrounding me. I walk through it and I step into a restaurant.

Someone is making a speech. I assume it is to a happy couple. At the main table, however, are two skeletons in wedding attire. Everyone else at the main table are skeletons dressed in formal wear.

I drag my eyes away from it and freeze when I see myself. Dimly, I recall that this is the wedding in Hawaii all those years ago. I walk over to the table where this new version of me is sitting. Bennett is flirting with a girl at the end of the table. My parents are talking in loud voices, recalling a story from a few years back. I am fiddling with a cheap camera I brought, trying to see if I can take some photos.

I hover behind myself. After a few seconds of deliberation, I try to rest my hand on myself. But my hand goes through me as if I am a ghost. Losing interest in myself fiddling with the camera, I look for Spencer.

She is exactly where she was in the photo. She is listening to Dad speak. I stand behind her, waiting for something to reveal itself. At one point, Kevin turns his head and whispers something in her ear. She laughs loudly and goes back to listening to Dad.

Is this it? I feel as if I can control the dream but when I left the wreckage, all it did was take me to the wedding from Hawaii. Growing frustrated, the dream starts to lose color. I look around wildly, hoping for something to jump out at me but —

I am sitting up in bed, gasping for air as if I have been underwater for too long. I rub my eyes and pinch my arm. The jolt of pain sends me crashing down. I am awake. I take a gulp of air. *You can't feel pain in dreams*, I tell myself. It was just another dream.

The bedsheets are tangled around my legs and I kick them off furiously. I try to control my breathing. The remains of the dream seem to settle on my skin, pricking at me. The wreckage is alive in my mind. Being trapped in the car, struggling to get out. The searing pain of my leg. I feel as if the walls are closing in on me.

I hear a noise. Someone is knocking. Still feeling panicked, I look at my clock. It is two in the morning. Who is knocking on my door at this time? The dream, like they always do, has left me feeling shaky and scared. I creep out of my bedroom toward the front door and hesitate.

I peek through the peephole and am shocked. I unlock the door quickly and open it.

"Bennett?" I say in surprise.

"Did I wake you?" he asks me.

I am taken aback at the fact he has shown up here at two in the morning. He looks disheveled. His hair is messy and for once he isn't wearing a suit jacket. The white dress shirt he has on shows off his muscles as usual, and his suit pants are wrinkled. He looks distressed which I have never seen so plainly on his face before. I certainly wasn't expecting Bennet to show up on my doorstep at this hour, especially looking like this.

"No, I just woke up from a dream. Are you okay?"

"I just didn't want to go back home. And I drove past your street and I just…" he shrugs, as if he has run out of words.

I let him in. There isn't any doubt that I wasn't going to let him in the apartment. Emily is away with Adam and I haven't seen Bennett look so stressed out before. *Layers and layers*, I think idly as he steps inside. I wonder what could have brought him to me. Even though we have slept together twice now, I still don't know where we stand. The animosity we had before has faded but is it friendship or is it something more between us?

"Do you want anything to drink?" I ask him, pushing those thoughts from my mind.

"Scotch." When he sees my face, he offers me a weak smile, "Joking. Water is fine."

I get some water for the two of us and sit next to him on the couch. He has turned the TV on and is flicking through the channels. Once in a while he runs his fingers through his hair. I let him enjoy the silence. I don't want to pressure him into speaking even though I am dying to know why he has come here.

After ten minutes of silence however, I realize that Bennett is content to just sit in my apartment and watch TV. Whatever desire he had to tell me about what is going on with him has faded. Finally, I put down the glass of water I am holding and look at him.

"Are you going to tell me why you didn't want to go back home?" I prompt him. "Not that I mind you coming by, but a reason would be nice."

"I tried telling Dad that I didn't want to pretend to be dating Stephanie anymore," Bennett says, not looking at me.

I mask my surprise and reply with, "I suppose Kevin wasn't too pleased with that."

"No. He's been planning all this shit with Stephanie's father, apparently. Not like he told me. I'm starting to think he was fine with me basically doing jack shit all these years because it meant I never thought about my future or where I was going. He always told me that I was going to take over the company and not to worry about anything else."

"And now?"

"Maybe he was fine with me just assuming I'll take control of the company because I never questioned anything. Because tonight – after I told him I didn't want to do anything else with Stephanie anymore – he flipped out. Just this cold rage. Not like anything I've seen from him before."

An unsettling feeling sits over me like a blanket. I suddenly wish I had a sweater on. The apartment feels cold. I must have left the AC low when I got home from the heat and fallen asleep without adjusting it. Goose bumps pop up along my skin. Bennett notices me shivering.

"You okay?"

"Yeah, cold, I guess."

The change of subject seems to snap Bennett out of his thoughts. "Man, coming by here so late… I'm sorry, April. Like you need this shit."

"It's okay, really," I tell him, thinking back to my dream. "I was awake anyway."

He hesitates and then leans back on the couch. He looks perturbed. For a second, I want to lean over and hug him but I hold back. Instead, I wait for him to talk again.

"Dad said that he has everything planned. That a merger between our company and Stephanie's company is going to be what is best for us. I asked him… why would we want to merge with a grocery store? That just pissed him off more. He started talking about how I have no business sense. How he should have reined me in before instead of letting me *run off to build cabins and join swim teams.*"

"That isn't true. I don't see the connection either. Kevin runs a media corporation. What would he get from owning grocery stores?"

"He told me he wants to branch out. He wants more than just his hands in the media. I guess news and tabloids aren't enough anymore. He wants to own grocery chains. He wants to buy up all sorts of different companies… wants his fingers in all the pies. Apparently, I'm supposed to just know this."

I think back to Kevin. Could I see him wanting that? *Definitely.* Kevin has always been the type of man who sets out to get more and more. He was never content to have just a little. A billion dollars was never enough. Growing the company was all he cared about. Yet…

"If he really thought he let you goof around too much, why didn't he stop it earlier?" I ask.

Bennett looks at me as if I started speaking another language.

"What I mean is, your father doesn't let anything slip by him. That's one of the reasons he is so good at making money. He sees business in every single movement. Do you really think if he thought you were a shitty heir to a mega-company he wouldn't have done something before now?"

"What are you saying?"

"I don't know. Maybe he was just mad at you for going against him. Emotional manipulation. So now you feel bad and you'll be more in line with going with whatever he says."

Bennett falls silent, clearly thinking about this. I wouldn't put it past Kevin to upset his son on purpose to make sure he doesn't speak out against dating Stephanie.

I speak up again. "Maybe Stephanie's father is only interested in a merger if you date her. So, if you don't date her, it'll muck up everything. Her father won't want to sell or go into business with Kevin. You're the key to all of this."

Bennett groans. "I don't want to date her anymore. She's so boring. She treats everything like a business transaction. I get that she has a guy she likes. That's fine. I don't care about that. But I just don't want to do it anymore."

"Why not?"

"What?"

"Why don't you? You seemed okay with it before. So… what changed?"

Bennett looks surprised that I asked such a thing. But I am curious. I keep finding out more and more about him. Small things, like how his father can upset him. Large things, like how he likes to work with his hands and create things. The Bennett of my childhood has been replaced by someone more complicated than I could ever have imagined.

"You, I guess," he mumbles so low that for a second, I think I imagine it.

"What?" I ask stupidly.

"You," he says louder and clears his throat. "Everything going on with you. I've just… I don't want to do it anymore. Whatever Dad wants. Maybe I don't even want to take over the company."

Every day seems to be growing weirder than the one before it. I open and close my mouth, unsure of what to say. I don't want to be mean, but I cannot imagine Bennett not having billions of dollars at his fingertips. It is hard having all these different pieces of him and being unsure of how to put them all together.

"What would you do?" I finally ask him, "without the company?"

"I don't know. I like to build things. I have my business degree from college. I'm not useless." He has an accusatory tone in his voice, as if he thinks I am mocking him.

"I'm not saying you can't do it," I tell him before he can grow upset. "I was just asking. But you're emotional right now too. Maybe you're just upset at Kevin…"

He leans over to me and grabs my hands. His skin is warm to the touch. My body reacts instantly to his touch even though there is nothing sexual about it. I realize I have been missing him.

"It isn't just that. April, what you're doing – you've always known what you've wanted to do. Even when things have happened. Even when you got into the accident. Even with how strange our families are. Yet you left it all behind. What if I take over Dad's company and I'm terrible at it? What if my dad is right? I don't know… I don't know what to do without the business. I have nothing to go off of except hobbies I like and some business experience." He hesitates. "What if Dad decides someone else should take over the company?"

"What? What in the world would make you think that? There isn't anyone else to take it over. You don't think he'd give it to Stephanie, do you? That's insane."

"No. I mean, maybe he wants me to date Stephanie to get that business merger, sure. But what if that is where my involvement stops?"

I study him, unsure of what to say. I pause for a moment and then move my hand to his cheek and brush it gently with my fingertips. Seeing Bennett so open and raw is a new feeling for me. It is strange to see him like this – exposed and scared. He closes his eyes briefly at my touch.

"You think he'd stick you with Stephanie, get the merger and be done with you?"

"Maybe."

"Who would take over the company then? Someone from his board?"

Bennett hesitates. He is on the verge of telling me something. I can see it in his eyes. He looks almost afraid, as if whatever he is going to tell me is something upsetting.

"Bennett?" I press.

He opens his mouth when suddenly my phone goes off. I had left it on the coffee table when I got home. The ringing noise shatters the mood between us as I jump, startled. I look over at it and see it is Spencer. My throat goes tight.

"Why is she calling you so late?" Bennett asks, looking afraid.

I reach for the phone, which suddenly feels like a million pounds, and answer the call.

"April?" Spencer's voice comes over from the other end, sounding hoarse.

"What?" I ask back brutally, already knowing the answer.

She lets out a choked sob, "Dad. It's Dad. April – he's – Dad is gone."

-To be continued in Book 3-

If you enjoyed this title, I would appreciate your leaving a review of the book. Good reviews encourage an author to write as well as help books to sell. Good reviews can be just a few short sentences describing what you liked about the book without having a spoiler. If you could spend 30 seconds writing a review, I would appreciate it: you can review this title right now at your favorite retailer.

Here is a preview of the **next story** you may also enjoy:

Torrid Exposure: A New Adult Romance Series - Book 3

THE WIND cuts through me like a knife. Even though it has been a hot summer, today is oddly chilly. As I walk out toward my car, I wish I had brought a sweater. The thought is an idle one. I would rather think about the cold than why I am out here.

"April!" a voice calls out to me.

I hesitate. For a brief moment, I want to ignore it. But I don't want to look rude. I stop and look behind me. It is an older man coming up to me now. In his suit and tie, I cannot place him. I am sure I have seen him before. He looks at me fondly as though he remembers me from when I was a little girl.

"April, I just wanted to tell you personally how sorry I am for the loss of your father," the man says to me. "It is a huge loss to everyone who knew him."

"Thank you very much," I say to him, the words tired of being repeated.

He smiles kindly at me. "I'm going to your mother's house for the wake. I'll see you there, dear."

The man walks past me. I watch him go. I have heard so many condolences today at my father's funeral that they are starting to blend together. They are sorry for my loss. My father was a great man. Everyone will miss him.

I blink rapidly, suddenly realizing my eyes are tearing up. I don't want to cry in front of all these strangers again. I cried when Dad's casket was lowered but how could I not? How could it be that Dad was here just a few days ago and now he is gone?

The last few days have felt like a blur. Spencer made the arrangements for the funeral because Mom went on a drinking binge right after he died. In spite of our bickering, I still reached out to Emily to tell her what was going on. She came back from where she had been with Adam as soon as she heard to be by my side, our fight forgotten. I hadn't seen Bennett since the night he had come over saying he wanted to get away from his father.

Spencer is waiting in the parking lot of the cemetery for Mom and me. I can see her now as I cut across the field, heading toward the parking lot. She is talking to Kevin. I don't see Bennett. Their heads are bowed close together and they both have dark looks on their faces. Something strikes me… it looks exactly how they looked that day I saw them bickering outside the hospital.

I find myself slowing down. Something is nagging me at the edge of my brain. It is as if something is trying to click into place. But between my grief and my stress, my brain is sluggish and slow to process anything. It is as if a fog has fallen across my brain.

"Hey!"

I look over to see Emily heading over to me. Whatever thoughts my brain was trying to assemble quickly vanish at the sight of her.

"Hey," I say back to her.

"How're you holding up?"

"Okay, I guess," I reply, although I don't even know if I feel okay.

Emily looks over her shoulder. "Your mom is talking to someone over there." She juts her chin over in the direction of where my mom is. "She said I could ride with you guys back home for the wake."

"Great," I reply, feeling relief at not being stuck in the limo with just Spencer and my mother.

Emily looks at me and concern is clear on her face. "April… I'm really sorry again, about what happened to your father. I really thought he was going to get better."

"No one was expecting the seizure," I tell her. "It happened quickly, at least. The seizure, plus the two strokes… it was all too much… he just…" My throat closes and I shrug, unable to say anything else.

Emily wraps her arms around me and pulls me in for a hug. I close my eyes and return it, trying to take comfort in the arms of my best friend. But I still feel empty and detached from everything going on around me.

"He loved you," she says in my ear. "He really did. I know when you backed out of the family business, Spencer and your mother didn't understand. But he did."

"I know," I reply, not wanting to cry.

Our conversation is interrupted when I see Spencer walking up to us. She is wearing all black. Her hair is down and flowing over her shoulders. She isn't wearing any make-up. Her skin is so pale that she looks sickly. There are bags underneath her eyes. I cannot remember the last time I saw Spencer with bags under her eyes.

"Hey, sorry. We have to get going now," she says to the two of us, her voice hollow.

I nod and together we get into the limo. Mom is already seated inside. She looks worse than Spencer and me put together. She sits in the back, wearing a bulky sweater that clings to her small frame. Even though it is dark inside the limo, she leaves her sunglasses on, which seem to swallow up her face. Her hair is piled messily on top of her head. Her skin is sallow and her face is tilted toward the window, looking out of it.

It is somewhat alarming to see Mom this way. Mom, who has always tended to drink a bit too much, always was able to keep it together. Now, however, one glance is all it takes to show that this is a woman who is letting control quickly slip through her fingers. She looks like a fragile broken doll at the back of the limo instead of a grieving widow.

Once we are all settled in, the limo heads toward the house for the wake. Part of me wishes I didn't have to stick around for it. It feels odd to stand around the house I no longer live in and discuss my father with business partners and people I do not know. My grief feels private and wholly my own.

No one speaks during the drive there. Mom is staring outside the window. Spencer is silently looking at her hands. I do not feel like speaking either. Emily opens a bottle of water from the mini-fridge and drinks it quietly. The silence feels suffocating. It is grief mingled with broken relationships amongst all of us. I can't stand it. I suddenly miss Dad more than ever.

As if sensing my thoughts, Spencer's eyes flick up to me. Our eyes meet. I wonder if she is thinking about a few days ago, when I came to her at the house, trying to patch things up. Dad's words echo in my mind. *Two sides of the same coin.* I had promised him that Spencer and I would make up.

Now that Dad is no longer here, I wonder if I will be able to keep that promise. It seemed impossible when I had sworn it. Now it feels as if it is my ultimate goal. Dad wants Spencer and me to be close sisters again. What do I have to do to make that happen? Do I have to simply let go of whatever happened that night of the accident and move on? Part of me wishes that I could. I just didn't know how to start letting that go.

Spencer finally looks away from me. I wonder what she is thinking about. As children, we were always on the same wavelength. Everything we did, it was on the same page. Now, I can't make a bet on what my sister is thinking.

"Spencer," my mom suddenly stirs, speaking up, "did you talk to Brian at the funeral?"

Brian, one of the investors who had alerted me that Dad's business was in trouble, hadn't bothered to glance at me at the funeral. Now that Dad is gone, Spencer is the one who has a firm reign on the company. I don't envy her. When I first heard that the company was in trouble, I had gone crazy, wanting to figure out how to resolve it. It took Bennett to make me realize I was just projecting my own concerns onto the company when it was no longer my business.

At the thought of Bennett, my thoughts grow more scattered. The boy I thought I had known has been replaced by a man I feel an intense pull toward. The billionaire playboy has hobbies that I never would have dreamt he would have had. It feels like a million years ago that Bennett had knocked on my door and had been upset about Kevin forcing him to basically *fake-date* Stephanie.

"Yes," Spencer replies, jarring me back to the present. "I did. Everything is under control. Don't worry about it, Mom."

This seems to placate her. She leans back in the seat and looks out the window again. The limo makes a turn and before I know it, we are pulling up to the house. Last time I had been here; Dad was still alive. I can't imagine going in the house now without him.

The limo parks and we get out of it, heading toward the house. People are already here and inside. Spencer is quickly swept up in a business conversation with someone I'm dimly aware of who works for the company. Emily holds onto my arm as we step inside the foyer of the house.

It is crowded. People who weren't invited to the funeral due to space have been invited to the wake. The house is quiet. Classical music is playing. We trail into the living room. The memories of times with my dad threaten to overwhelm me. I wish the house were empty and that I could walk through it by myself. My throat feels closed.

"Do you want anything to drink?" Emily whispers.

"Water, please," I manage to choke out.

She nods, promises me she will be back soon, and heads off toward the kitchen. I position myself near one of the windows, focusing on where the trees meet the bright blue sky. I trace the outline of the trees, hoping it will calm me down. I feel nervous and jittery, as if I am on the verge of a panic attack.

Emily returns with a glass of water and says, "This place is crowded. Your mom is talking to someone in the kitchen and is already hitting the wine."

Her voice is casual but I know what she is saying. It is only a matter of time until mom is too drunk to function. People will excuse it today. She is grieving, after all. But Emily knows what I know. Mom was already drinking increasingly when Dad was alive. Now that he is gone, what will stop her from going over the edge?

"April," Emily says to me and runs her fingers through her hair, "I'm sorry about… us fighting… about Adam and everything."

The fact she is dating Adam again and hid it from me feels so small and pointless that I have barely thought about it since she came home.

"Emily," I say, my voice sounding distant, "I have to tell you something too."

"What?"

"I've slept with Bennett. Twice."

Emily looks alarmed at this. I can't tell if she is alarmed at the fact that I have slept with Bennett, or that I have neglected to tell her, or that I am telling her now, of all times. She steps toward me and takes hold of my arm. Her voice is barely above a whisper now.

"April, what? Like… after your father died? Because I understand… you're emotional and everything is upsetting…"

I appreciate the fact she is trying to give me a way out but I shake my head. "No. The day after the summer party and one of the nights you were working late… or seeing Adam, I guess."

Her eyes are as wide as saucers. If I didn't feel so empty, I would have found it funny. How could Emily not be surprised? Bennett and I had never gotten along. Now here I am telling her that we have slept together twice.

"Oh," she says, looking lost. "Are you… I mean, like, dating? Isn't he seeing that Stephanie woman? I didn't know…"

"We aren't seeing each other. I don't know what we are doing," I admit.

Saying it out loud feels strangely liberating. It is true. I don't know what Bennett and I are doing. Even though I have stepped away from the money and the company, I still find myself in Bennett's circle. When I am around him, I cannot help but feel drawn to him. The revelations about him have changed how I thought about him before. Bennett is like quicksand… the more I struggle to get away from him, the more I feel myself fall deeper.

Emily blinks. "You don't know?"

"No," I confirm. "It's confusing at the moment."

"I'm just surprised, that's all," she says. "I mean, obviously, who you sleep with is totally your own judgment but…"

I know what she is thinking. Emily doesn't want to cast any judgment on me because she knows we just fought about her dating Adam again.

"It's okay," I tell her. "I'm not really thinking about it right now."

Our conversation is interrupted by a long train of people giving me their condolences. Most of the people I have spoken to over the years in passing, that is, until I opted out of ever working in the family business.

There is one person that I see on the opposite side of the room that I want to speak to, however. James is here. I had seen him briefly at the funeral but he seemed to be keeping a low profile. Even though he quit the company shortly before Dad's death, I know that he is hurting as much as I am. He adored my father.

Excusing myself from a conversation with two people I barely recall meeting a few years ago, I head across the room toward him. Emily watches me leave but doesn't go after me. James is hovering by a plate of finger sandwiches, although he hasn't taken one.

"James, hi," I say to him.

He looks up at me. He appears to have aged forty years since I last saw him. His face is etched with lines and he is going gray. Even so, his smile lights up his face at seeing me.

"April. A pleasure to see you."

"Same here. Been a while," I tell him, taking one of the finger sandwiches and nibbling on it.

He follows my lead, taking one as well, and together we trail away from the table and out of the main living room. We end up in one of the smaller sitting areas where Dad kept some of his books. There is only a small group of people here across from us. We sit down on a couch.

"I'm crushed by the death of Richard," James says softly. "I don't think I need to explain why."

"No, you don't. Dad always spoke very highly of you. He loved you like a brother." My throat feels tight again and I look down at the small sandwich in my hand.

James sighs. "I feel as if I abandoned him at the end. Quitting like that. I should have stuck around… maybe…"

"Maybe, what? He wouldn't have had that seizure? You can't start thinking like that," I say firmly. "There was nothing you could have done. Dad didn't even know you quit. He wasn't exactly all there at the end."

James looks at me. His eyes look grey, like stormy seas.

"Thank you. I hope in time that lessens the guilt I feel."

A few days ago, if I had a chance to speak to James, I would have tried to grill him about the status of the company. Why did he quit? What was my mom meddling about? But today, I cannot find the energy. It is Spencer's problem now.

"Richard was a great man. I hated leaving. I hope you know that. I tried to tell your sister that I didn't want to leave. They wanted me to take over, you know. Help Spencer learn the ropes in case your father passed away. But I couldn't."

"Spencer should be okay," I tell him.

"Maybe…," he hesitates. "I'd feel better if Kevin wasn't her mentor though, to be honest."

If you enjoyed this sample then look for **Torrid Exposure: A New Adult Romance Series - Book 3**.

Here is a preview of **another story** you may also enjoy:

Fifty Recipes For Disaster: A New Adult Romance Series - Book 2

"**HOW LONG** on the spot prawns, Chef Kiara?" Robbs asks me with mock reverence from across the kitchen. Two months have passed since I was awarded the apprentice position at Fission. Paul Weston stayed out of the decision. No one was able to outright accuse him of being biased and giving the job to his girlfriend, but the rumors are swirling. The rumors about how I landed my job are the least of my problems, though. Paul and Jenny's upcoming arrival is what really has everyone talking around here.

Every time I think of that fateful morning at Paul's appointment, I'm overwhelmed with the same sick feeling in the pit of my stomach. When Paul called me out of the hallway that morning, Jenny bawled and apologized over and over again. She even offered to get rid of the baby, but Paul and I were against it. Paul had immediately insisted an abortion wasn't an option. I agreed with him, but I still can't wrap my head around the idea that in roughly six months, my boyfriend will have a child with another woman. This wasn't supposed to happen, and I'm helpless to do anything about it.

When the apprenticeship contest ended, Jenny left Fission. It's easier for me to deal with her now that I don't see her every day. Paul spent a lot of time reassuring me that I'm the woman he loves, but a part of me doesn't trust him. Family is important to Paul… he'll want to be a hands-on type of dad, and being with Jenny would make that possible.

A year ago, I'd have never been in this position. The situation unfolding before me is a perfect example of why I never let anyone through my walls. But there is something about Paul that made me drop my guard. I am in love with him, and if this baby is going to be a part of his life then I guess it'll be a part of mine, too. I just hope Jenny keeps a lid on all of the 'baby mama drama.'

"Chef?" Robbs calls loudly and brings my focus back to the present.

"Prawns will be up in three," I tell him.

Never having to put up with Robbs Martin again was what I'd been most looking forward to at the end of the apprenticeship competition. But two days before the contest was over, Paul's prep cook Ernesto gave his notice. Ernesto and his wife had just given birth, and he'd been offered a better paying job that would allow him more time off with his family. Paul was overwhelmed and had no time or patience to interview for a new hire. Before the results of the competition were announced, he opened the prep cook position for one of the runners up. Jenny had already decided to leave Fission and take some time to decide what she really wants to do. Robbs was awarded the job by default. I'd expected the bitchy attitude he'd had during the contest to carry over into his new job, but so far he's actually been pleasant to work with. He shows up on time, he helps the other chefs once his tasks are finished, and he makes friendly conversation while doing so. I'm enjoying his new work attitude, but I still don't trust him any farther than I can throw him. Robbs already showed me his true colors, and I don't give people second chances... except for Paul, that is.

I pull the prawns from the grill, plate them, and carry them to Robbs' station. He sets them next to the vegetables he's already prepped for tonight's seafood chowder.

"Did you toss the shells and tails into the stock pot?" Robbs asks me, as if I don't know what I'm doing.

"Of course I did," I answer politely. I can't stand the guy, but I'm not going to give him the satisfaction of letting him get to me.

"Thanks, Chef," he says with a fake smile.

I nod at him and return to my station. I'm doing an appetizer special tonight, and I need to get everything prepped. I prefer to do my own knife work, instead of relying on Robbs. *I have plenty of time for prep work. It's kind of hard to be a chef's apprentice when the chef is never here...*

The toll Jenny's pregnancy took on my job was even harder than the toll it was taking on my personal life. Paul is constantly leaving work to go to doctor's appointments or to shop for cribs. Once he left just because Jenny was craving cheese soup from Mamma's Kettle and was too tired to leave her apartment to pick it up. I had a lot of freedom in the kitchen, but I fought for the job to *learn* from Paul, not to cover for him.

I can't let myself drown in frustration. Not when a lot of work needs to be done. I fill three stock pots with water and set them to boil on the stove. To one I add cumin, cinnamon, and chili powder. The second gets saffron and kefir limes, while the third is seasoned with basil and rosemary. The pots begin to boil, so I toss a handful of salt into each, add my rice, and carefully replace the lids. I turn off the burners and turn my attention to my proteins. I'm making a sushi trio inspired by different areas of the world. I want to do a marinated beef tartar for the Latin roll, but I'm still torn between a couple of different fish for the Indian and the Mediterranean. I need to consider our stock of each of the fish, so I set off for the walk-in cooler.

"Chef Kiara?" a voice calls from behind me. I turn and see Megan, one of the hostesses, standing in the kitchen doorway.

"What is it now?" I groan.

If you enjoyed this sample then look for **Fifty Recipes For Disaster: A New Adult Romance Series - Book 2**.

Here is a preview of **another story** you may enjoy:

Alpha Infiltration: A Paranormal Shifter Romance Series - Book 2 by Darla Dunbar

"**YOU LOOK** awfully chipper this morning," Jason Traverse said to his twin when she strolled through the front door.

"Why shouldn't I be?" Sarina asked. She quirked an eyebrow at him as if to emphasize her point.

"Being pregnant, I'd think you'd be miserable," Jason smirked. "At least I sort of hoped you would be."

"Jerk," she said, teasing. Rounding the corner, Sarina greeted her mother, who was already up preparing breakfast.

"All grown up and still the bickering never stops," Amanda Walker-Traverse said, grinning at her daughter. "You do look lovely Sarina."

"At least someone in the family knows beauty when they see it."

"You get it from me, so it's only natural that I would," her mom said, laughing. "How's Brody?"

"Running around like a mad wolf. He seems to think these two will grow fast like Jason and I did."

"Well, werewolves do tend to grow much faster than their human counterparts," Amanda said, giving Sarina a gentle reminder.

"I know," she agreed. "I just don't think we need to baby proof the house today, or have a nursery ready yesterday. Brody insists on it so I just stay out of his way.”

“I’m happy to know that he cares so much for you,” Amanda said with a smile. “I have to admit there was a time, not so long ago, that we all worried that you’d made a mistake. Then, when you went through that period of forgetting when none of us knew who Brody was, it was just odd. Now that everything’s back to normal, I can take a step back and tell you that you chose wisely. It was brash to say the least, but you knew your mate and never faltered from that decision.”

“Thanks, Mama. Now if only Jason here could find himself a mate.”

“Who says I haven’t?” Jason said defensively. “I have a woman in mind. It just so happens not all of us are ready to jump on the matrimonial bandwagon as of yet.”

“Oh please,” Sarina scoffed. “I’ll take my dying breath before you ever take a mate. You’d much rather just take a woman to your bed without all the trappings of a relationship. I know.”

“I’m not denying that having a woman in my bed is nice, but lately I’ve come to realize that there’s more to life than a couple of hours of passion in the night.”

“Welcome to reality little brother,” Sarina smiled.

“Can you two please talk about something other than sex at eight in the morning?” Amanda said.

Sarina took a seat close to her brother and thanked her mother for the French toast she'd been served. "This is amazing."

"You always say that," Amanda chuckled.

"That's because I'm always right," Sarina winked. "These two want more." She gestured to her belly.

"I was ravenous when I was carrying you two," Amanda said. Sarina watched her mother with a smile on her face. She'd taken her mother for granted, that much she knew. Still stunning at almost fifty in human years, Amanda was a picture of beauty. The way she moved showed strength and grace. Her hair still lustrous and dark as mahogany. Her eyes still sparkled when she smiled, which she did often, especially if the children's father was close by. "I'm surprised your father didn't kick me out when I got pregnant with Wade."

"Please," Sarina laughed. "Daddy's been crazy about you since day one. I've never seen any signs of that changing. If I didn't know better, I'd say you two are still on your honeymoon."

"We are darling," Amanda laughed. "Well, maybe not, but we're still over the moon about each other and we both know it. When you choose a mate there is no other who can turn your head."

"You're getting awfully sentimental on us in your old age, Mother," Jason teased. One look from her had him clearing his throat and stuffing his mouth with French toast.

"Careful now, pup," Romeo said with a grin as he entered the kitchen. "Old age or not, I'd still lay money on your mother to give you a good ass whoopin'."

"Yeah, yeah," Jason said with a wary smile.

Sarina loved these moments. It was one of the many things she'd miss now that she and Brody had finally finished moving everything into the home he'd been given when he'd conceded his leader status. Brody, Sarina's mate, had killed Reggie, the former alpha of his pack and taken over, all with the sensible intentions of bringing his pack under the tutelage and ruling right of Romeo and Amanda. As King and Queen of the Delta packs, it was only right that his pack join them. Since doing so, his pack had wanted for little and seemed even more settled than he'd ever seen them. Instead of living in caves like dogs, he was happy to report to Sarina and everyone else that his former pack was elated with how things turned out. They'd been given homes, food, necessities of everyday life and overall, they'd been well taken care of.

Brody, in exchange for his submission, had been given prominent status within the pack as a general. He helped Romeo keep the pack together and content, working as a liaison for those who lived further away from New Delta, making sure everyone had the necessities they needed. For her part, Sarina was happy to be pampered as her unborn twins continued to grow strong and rather quickly. She wasn't sure they were developing as fast as she and Jason had, but she was already showing and they'd only found out about the babies a month ago. At the rate she was going, it'd be well under half of the normal human pregnancy term when she would be ready to deliver. No wonder werewolves multiplied so quickly.

<<<>>>

Finding her mother after breakfast, Sarina voiced her concerns. "I'm thinking about asking Brody if we should stay near the hospital from April on until the babies arrive."

"That's not a bad idea, although having them at home isn't a bad option either. I learned a lot about myself when I was having you. I found a confidence and reliance on myself and the ones I love. I probably wouldn't have noticed had I not been able to deliver you as I did."

"It's scary this first time."

"It's always a little bit of an anxious time, although I will say the first time there is always the unknown. I will support you in whatever you decide, Sarina."

"I'll see what Brody says and let you know from there."

"You do that, sweetheart. Meanwhile, I've got some major craft projects to get started if we're going to have these babies taken care of when the time comes. Never let anyone tell you twins don't run in families."

<<<>>>

Fenris sat back and contemplated his next move. Sending the young buck, Brandt, to seduce and impregnate Romeo's eldest had been a stroke of genius on his part. Now to wait and see if the seed she carried belong to Brandt or her worthless wolf of a mate. Fenris was already smiling, just thinking about it. It wouldn't truly matter of course. He'd rip them apart no matter whose seed she carried.

He'd thought long and hard over the last several weeks about how to go about his first strike. He wanted it to hurt… a lot. Romeo needed to know and understand that he was not the alpha in charge. It wouldn't be easy, as taking down any alpha never was, but Fenris knew that given the alternative, Romeo would bow his knee to him.

He could almost see that moment and could admit that it turned him on. Having the play of any female he wished, including Romeo's sweet wife, or even one of his succulent daughters. Brandt had howled for days about the one called Sarina and how beautiful she was. Fenris couldn't blame him for getting hooked on her. An alpha's daughter was no small prize and if she was beautiful and put out as hotly as Brandt proclaimed, Fenris himself might even give her some enviable attention.

At any rate, Fenris knew that his first strike had to be the hardest and most elusive. If he did it right, and he damn well would, Romeo Traverse and his family would have no choice but to submit to his ruling. The thought of ruling the entire Delta area sent a ripple of fire through his blood as he thought about making the Traverse family pay. They'd been a thorn in his side ever since they'd split from his line. Now he'd finally worked out a plan that would set things right. He could hardly wait to get started.

"Dankar!" Fenris shouted. His patience, he could admit, wore thin during times when he was thinking about what was coming.

"You called for me sir?"

"I need you to do whatever it is you did to Brandt again. It needs to be perfect and if you can manage a longer time, that'd be in your best interest as well."

"I'll get right on it, sir."

"See that you do."

Brandt met Dankar in his quarters. "You wanted to see me, Dankar?"

"Yes, yes," the small man said. "Come, sit."

Brandt did as he was bade and sat in the chair where Dankar had worked on him the last time. "I presume that Fenris wanted you to make me like Brody again?"

"Yes," Dankar replied, his tone short.

"Remember, Dankar, you may be Fenris' right hand man, but it is I who watches your back. Show some damn respect."

"Yes, Brandt," said Danker, but guardedly this time.

Brandt watched the little man mix potions and concoctions of who-knew-what brew. The noxious fumes were almost enough to make him pass out. He hoped that whatever it was that Dankar was doing, that it worked well and fast, because the last thing he wanted was to have to drink some nasty shit.

"This may not feel nice," Dankar said to him as he injected him with a large dose of some neon fluid. "But it should let you have an uninterrupted two weeks with Sarina and her family. Don't screw it up"

Brandt went back to his room and awaited the change he knew was coming. The first time had been less than pleasant as his body shifted into that of the alpha's daughter's mate. He'd had twenty-four hours last time. If he had to account for fourteen days, this was going to royally suck. Like most synthetic drugs it took nearly twenty minutes to feel the effects, but once they started, Brandt could hardly breathe. Even going from man to wolf, his change always started in his eyes.

Pain shot through his irises and into his optic nerves as brown turned to blue and his pupils dilated. With his pupils the size of dimes, he was thankful his room had no windows. The light he had forgotten to shut off streamed into his vision, making Brandt curse as he swiped a hand down the wall, desperately trying to find the switch. "Shit!" he growled as his body, relentless under the pressure of the drug's interference, continued its change. His shoulders widened and his torso and legs lengthened. The muscles in his arms, thighs and abdomen stretched and added new tissue as his body grew from a modest five foot eleven, to the taller

Brody, who easily stood six foot, three inches. His jaw cracked and widened, giving him the strong jawline Brody sported. The hair on his head grew thicker, sprouting thousands of new hairs to add the lush texture of Brody's dark locks.

Two hours after it had all begun, Brandt was finally able to look in the mirror and see Brody standing there. His eyes, now crystal blue, smiled when he did. The facial hair, dark in texture and color, much like his hair, was easy to shave. He knew from watching, that Brody rarely wore a beard or let his facial hair grow much past a five o'clock shadow. He scowled, smiled, frowned and made every facial expression he could think of to make sure the process had changed his physical appearance in every way.

"It looks as if all went well," Dankar said, standing in Brandt's doorway.

"Screw you," Brandt said, glaring at Dankar. "The only solace I have is that I have two weeks to forget the pain. I may want to kill you when I change back. Be mindful to keep your distance from me when I do."

"I won't forget," Dankar said. Brandt could have sworn a grin crossed the man's face. If he didn't know better, he'd lay money on the pain being the most enjoyable part for Dankar when he concocted his potions. He had yet to use one that didn't have some sort of pain with it.

If you enjoyed this sample then look for **Alpha Infiltration: A Paranormal Shifter Romance Series - Book 2 by Darla Dunbar**.

Other Books by Carla Coxwell

- Torrid Exposure New Adult Romance Series

- Devil's Advocate BBW MC New Adult Romance Series

- Fifty Recipes For Disaster New Adult Romance Series

- Star Bright New Adult Romance Series (This series follows "Fifty Recipes For Disaster New Adult Romance Series")

- Obsessed Bounty Hunter Romance Series

Get the latest update on new releases from the author at:

https://www.carlacoxwell.com/newsletter

About the Author - Carla Coxwell

Carla has always been a fan of romance novels. To augment what she made waiting on tables to help her way through college, Carla also did some freelance work in the romance genre.

Now she enjoys living vicariously through her characters in her New Adult Romance books.

Connect with Carla Coxwell

I really appreciate you reading my book! Here are my social media coordinates:

Friend me on Facebook: https://www.facebook.com/CarlaCoxwell/

Follow me on Twitter: https://twitter.com/carlacoxwell

Check me out on Goodreads: https://www.goodreads.com/author/show/10691544.Carla_Coxwell

Subscribe to my newsletter: https://www.carlacoxwell.com/newsletter/

Visit my website: https://www.carlacoxwell.com/